MW01041253

THE WELL-HEELED MURDERS

THE
WELL-HEELED
MURDERS

CHERRY HARTMAN

Spinsters Ink
Duluth

The Well-Heeled Murders ©1996 by Cherry Hartman
All rights reserved

First edition
10-9-8-7-6-5-4-3-2

Spinsters Ink
32 E. First St., #330
Duluth, MN 55802-2002

This is a work of fiction. Any similarity to persons living or dead is a coincidence.

Cover art by Julie Delton
Cover design by Gail Wallinga

Production: Helen Dooley   Lori Loughney
               Joan Drury   Jami Snyder
               Emily Gould   Amy Strasheim
               Claire Kirch   Liz Tufte
               Kelly Kager   Nancy Walker

Library of Congress Cataloging-in-Publication Data
Hartman, Cherry
     The well-heeled murders / Cherry Hartman — 1st ed.
        p.   cm.
ISBN 1-883523-10-9 (alk. paper)
     I. Title.
PS3558.A7117W45   1996
813'.54—dc20   96–9221
                                                    CIP

Printed on recycled paper

For Judith Barrington and the 29th Street Writers Group:

Karen Brummel-Smith
Elissa Goldberg
Kathleen Haley
Kathleen Herron
Mary Henning-Stout
Andee Hochman
Janet Howey
Shirley Kishiyama
Mimi Maduro
Amy Schutzer
Ila Suzanne

1

Quietly, Morgan put her ear to Victoria's office door. She heard muffled sobs. With a sigh, Morgan lowered herself onto a velvet settee. She craned her neck to catch her reflection in a wall mirror, ran her fingers through her brown curls, checked her eye shadow, and looked around the prim waiting room. Every available surface held a bouquet of flowers and a box of Kleenex. Since losing her only child, Dr. Victoria Trimbell had become a grief counselor. Morgan noticed the door on the opposite side of the room was slightly ajar.

The partially open door intrigued her. No therapist would ever dream of conducting a session without the door being tightly sealed for reasons of confidentiality. During breaks, a therapist wouldn't want to be viewed by her office mate's clients—it might cause some havoc with transference. Morgan picked up a copy of *Modern Maturity* and tried to engross herself in an article on "The Sexual World of Octogenarians," but her mind kept wandering back to the open door.

She had never been formally introduced to Victoria's office mate, Dr. Lucinda Frazier, but she had seen her several times at various mental health meetings. Morgan, too, was a clinical psychologist. She specialized in women's issues, although recently she had cut her practice to half time in order to teach graduate courses on the feminist practice of psychotherapy.

"I could just knock and introduce myself," she decided. She slowly approached and rapped twice on the dark oak door. No answer. Morgan knocked again. Nothing. Hesitantly, she pushed the door forward.

There was no need to introduce herself. Dr. Frazier was dead. The middle-aged woman lay on her back on a Freudian-style leather couch. Her gray woolen dress was bunched up around her waist, and her panty hose were tightly wrapped around her throat.

It occurred to Morgan to remove the panty hose and administer mouth-to-mouth resuscitation, even though it was clear to her that Dr. Frazier's fate had been sealed at least a couple of hours earlier. But she let years of reading mystery novels guide her next actions. Careful not to touch anything and squelching her impulse to pull Dr. Frazier's dress down, Morgan left the office, walked across the waiting room, and pounded on Victoria's door.

"Morgan! I'm still in session. I'll be with you . . ."

"No time, Vic." Ignoring the small man with tears streaming down his face, Morgan boldly strode into the room, picked up the phone, dialed 911, and reported the murder.

"I don't understand why you couldn't have called from Lucinda's, Morgan. This has really upset poor Mr. Meyers," complained Victoria while they were waiting for the police to arrive.

"Fingerprints, Vic. The killer may have left his or hers on the phone. I'm sorry about Mr. Meyers. I can imagine how upsetting it must be for him to know he's sitting across the hall from a murder scene. I'm feeling a little squeamish myself."

Victoria glanced at her closed office door. "It isn't the

murder that bothers him as much as you seeing him cry. He doesn't cry in public. It would have helped if you could have just let him quietly leave before the police got here. I'm sure he doesn't have any useful information, and he doesn't want his wife to *know* he's in therapy." Victoria blinked back tears. "Oh, I don't even *know* what I'm talking about, I'm so upset about Lucinda."

Morgan looked at her friend. Large, almond-shaped eyes dominated Victoria's face. They were larger than usual. Her straight, black hair was in its customary, meticulous French knot. Her peach-colored skin, inherited from her Korean father and Inuit mother, had paled.

Just then, two uniformed police officers followed by a burly man in a suit and another one wearing glasses came into the waiting room.

"Who reported a homicide?" Glasses asked.

"I did," Morgan responded, leading the group into Lucinda Frazier's office.

"Wait outside!" Burly barked. As she retreated, Morgan noticed that Dr. Frazier's shoes were missing. Her eyes went from the victim's bare feet to the end of the couch and swept across the floor before the door was shut in her face. No shoes.

The next hour was spent answering the questions of Detective Reynolds (Glasses) and Detective Perry (Burly). Morgan gave a straightforward account of discovering the body. She mentioned the missing shoes, but the detectives didn't seem interested. A team of technicians was setting up lights for photographs and dusting for prints when Morgan was asked to reenact her movements in Dr. Frazier's office.

Victoria told the detectives that she hadn't seen Lucinda that day, which wasn't unusual because Victoria was on an hourly schedule and Dr. Frazier saw clients on the half hour. "We've shared the office space about two years. Occasionally we lunch together, but we're not really close friends."

"Do you discuss cases?" Detective Reynolds asked.

"No. Actually, I couldn't if I wanted to. Ethically, I can only discuss clients with members of my peer group. Morgan is in my group."

"Anyone you know want to see her dead?" Detective Reynolds asked while chewing his knuckle.

"I, I . . . don't know any voyeurs," Victoria stammered. Reynolds gave her a blank look.

"Oh, I see what you mean," Victoria recovered. "Well, lots of clients have ambivalent feelings toward their therapists, but she hasn't mentioned any particular problems lately. I know she's separated from her husband, but I don't think it's a hostile separation. Her son is away at college . . ." Victoria's voice broke at this point, and Morgan knew Vic was thinking of her own dead son, Wendell.

Lucinda went by in a body bag on a trolley. Victoria phoned and cancelled her afternoon clients. Morgan watched the uniformed police seal off the psychologist's office. Detective Perry was off interviewing other building tenants to see if anyone had seen or heard anything unusual.

When Victoria returned, Detective Reynolds said, "We'll probably be questioning both of you again. Let us know if you're going to leave town or if you think of anything important." He handed each of them his card. Out of habit, Morgan reached into her purse and gave him one of hers.

As they took the elevator down to the lobby, Morgan again noticed that Victoria's skin seemed drained. She tried to get in touch with her own feelings, but she drew a blank. Adrenaline numbness, she decided. "We still have to eat," she said to Victoria. "Let's try Luigi's." They hurried along the wet sidewalks of downtown Portland, Oregon, on this blustery March day, silently fighting to keep the wind from carrying away their umbrellas or turning them inside out.

When they were settled into a comfortable booth, they ordered chiles rellenos and fajitas. Luigi, a huge man of Italian ancestry, often joked that he had learned to cook in the Mexican Navy. Morgan didn't know if there even was a Mexican Navy, but the tortilla chips were always fresh and warm, and there were plenty of vegetarian items on the menu.

Sipping her mineral water, Morgan noticed that Victoria was putting one chip after another in her mouth, not even pausing to dip into the salsa. Her eyes were wide and glazed. "Vic! Slow up! You know Luigi limits us to two baskets."

"I feel sort of weird, Morgan. It could have been me."

"What do you mean, Vic?"

"Well, if some crazy just walked in off the street, he could have just as easily come into my office as Lucinda's. Or, if it was a client gone berserk, well, I work with a lot of rageful people. Oh, God! I don't want to be scared of my clients, Morgan!" Despite her stylish black suit and sophisticated hairstyle, Victoria looked very young.

"This is scary, Vic." Morgan was trying to erase the sight of Dr. Frazier's bulging eyes and slate-gray face from her mind and attend to her friend. "But I doubt that it was some stranger off the street, and the fact that it happened in her office may be a red herring."

"What do you mean?"

"Maybe someone wanted the police to believe it was a client. I think most victims are actually murdered by people close to them—spouses, children. This probably has something to do with Lucinda Frazier herself. Tell me about her, Vic." Morgan asked in an effort to distract Victoria from her panic and prevent her from letting the shock take her into a fresh round of grieving for her dead son.

"She moved to Portland a couple of years ago from the East Coast. Her husband's a big honcho with some multinational company and they transferred him here. She was upset about leaving her practice and starting over. Maybe that's why they split. I don't know. She was very private about the details. Oh, God! I'm starting to talk about her in the past tense!" Victoria was fighting tears. She opened her purse and dug through several pockets before her hand emerged with a clean, pressed hanky.

"It's okay, Vic," reassured Morgan. Luigi eyed them from the bar. "Did Lucinda specialize in any particular kind of client?"

"She had a general practice, but I know she was particularly interested in sexual deviancy." Morgan raised an eyebrow. "Not sex offenders. Fetishes, cross-dressing, that kind of thing."

"Hmmmmm. This could be important. Maybe we should tell one of those detectives."

"How about the cute one with glasses?" Vic teased, recovering some of her equilibrium.

"Hardly my type."

"Maybe if you imagined him with longer hair, breasts . . ."

"You should know I'm a one-woman woman, Victoria Trimbell."

Victoria winked. "Maybe one at a time is more your style, Morgan McRain. And, let's see, you and April have been together just about five years now. That's pushing your limit, sweetie. Besides, just because you've never tried men doesn't mean you never will."

"Talk like that'll get you thrown out of the lesbian union, Vic."

12

"Morgan! Wake up!" April elbowed her partner in the ribs. "Phone for you."

"Hmmph! What time is it? What's wrong?" Morgan grumbled into the phone.

"Morgan, it's 6 o'clock, for heaven's sake. Nothing's wrong. I thought you'd be up."

"It's Wednesday, Vic. You know I always take Wednesday off. April's staying home this morning, too, so we can . . . have a leisurely breakfast." Morgan glanced in April's direction. Her fine, blonde hair was the only thing showing out of the covers. She was feigning snores.

"In case you forgot, Lucinda Frazier's funeral is today at two. I really need you to go with me for moral support." There was a long pause, which Morgan didn't fill. Victoria continued, "You know, since Wendell's death, I have a hard time with funerals."

"Geez, Vic, you're the only grief counselor I know who's funeral-phobic." Morgan took a deep breath. Wendell had been the victim of a drive-by shooting three years before. Morgan sometimes felt angry with her friend for not being able to let go and get on with her life. At the same time, she couldn't imagine her own life without Priscilla Roxanne, April's three-year-old. Morgan's voice softened, "Sure. I'll go, Vic. Pick me up here."

"Good news, April. We have plenty of time for breakfast in bed and out of bed." Morgan ran her tongue lightly around April's ear.

※ ※ ※

"Pancakes! Pancakes! Pancakes!" Priss sang as she ran to embrace April and Morgan as they arrived arm in arm in the large blue-and-white kitchen. April had on a pin-striped "power" suit with all the accessories appropriate to lawyering. Morgan contrasted in a pink-and-green jogging suit with eye shadow to match. Morgan never wore make-up, except eye shadow. She considered her violet-blue eyes to be her best feature, and she made the most of them. As usual, her brown curly hair hadn't been combed.

"Coffee's brewed, and these are just about ready," called Donald, flipping a flapjack high in the air. April's twenty-six-year-old brother lived over their detached garage. Besides being an important part of the family, he was chief cook and bottle washer and Priss's full-time nanny.

April gave her brother a hug and a kiss as Morgan helped Priss get settled onto a stack of telephone books. Priss had recently declared that high chairs were for babies. "I'm not a baby. I'm a big girl," was a frequently heard statement. "Don't tell me 'no'" had been her first complete sentence.

Morgan gazed fondly at her partner, April Daley. She had the kind of silky blonde hair that could only be worn very short or very long because it refused to hold a style. Her blue-green eyes outshone her pale face and small features. They were deep set with a sparkle reserved only for Priss and Morgan.

"I won't be able to relieve you this afternoon, if that's okay with you," Morgan said to Donald as he handed her a plate of pancakes with ricotta cheese and sliced oranges. "I have to go to a funeral. I hope that works for you. Maybe Priss and I can take a walk when I get home."

"No problem. I didn't have any definite plans." Donald flipped another pancake into the air. "Maybe this is a good day to try a new recipe for modeling dough with Priss. I read about Dr. Frazier's murder in the paper. Do the police have any leads?"

"I haven't heard anything. Maybe Victoria will have some news." Morgan gobbled another bite.

"What's a foo rawl?" Priss was dividing oranges and pieces of pancake into separate piles on her plate.

"That's when you say good-bye to someone who's died." April believed in being honest with her daughter. "Remember when we did that with Timmy Turtle before we flushed him down the toilet? Remember we told him how much we loved him and would miss him?"

"What's modeling dough?" Priss's attention had moved on.

"It's like clay. We can make animals and stuff," enthused Donald.

"Can I make a turtle?"

3

Morgan sat very still. Although not as tense as poor Vic, who was shredding a pile of Kleenex into her lap, she hated funeral parlors. She was always relieved when a memorial service was held outside or, as was becoming more popular with her friends in this age of AIDS, in someone's home. Morgan was tempted to begin an essay in her head about how having large numbers of people die in their twenties, thirties, and forties was changing American death practices. However, she pulled herself back to the present by focusing on the stairway to heaven painted on the wall ahead of her, in front of which sat a huge mahogany casket.

"Doesn't her family have enough environmental awareness to avoid tropical woods?" she fretted silently. "Good Goddess, it's hard to stay in this room." She turned to stare at the wall beside her, which was lined with floor-to-ceiling glass cases filled with stuffed dead animals arranged in forest scenes.

"How are you doing, Vic?" Morgan asked.

"I'm okay." Victoria started gathering up the little bits of tissue and wadding them into a ball. "Thank God the casket is closed. I'm pretty sure that's her husband and her son in the front row. I've seen the boy's picture on her desk."

Morgan looked in the direction of Victoria's nod and saw a man in his fifties with salt-and-pepper hair, in an expensive, dark suit sitting beside a fidgeting young man with his head bowed. Funeral music swelled from beneath the hands of an elderly organist, and two ushers walked down the center aisle and raised the coffin lid. A brass bracket, like one that holds up the hood on a car, kept the lid propped open, apparently so Lucinda could view the ceremony. Morgan was close enough to see that the gray pallor had been covered over with beige skin tones and rouge thick enough to give Dr. Frazier the appearance of one of Madame Toussaud's creations.

Milling about in the foyer afterwards with teacup in one hand and cookie in the other, Morgan was bumped from behind by Dr. Lance Rogers, a clinical psychologist she knew slightly. "So sorry. Have you seen Maude? I need to get back for my four o'clock."

"She's over in the corner talking with Darrell Richardson and Corky Vanderpelt." Morgan pointed them out. She and Maude Ross had a long history of mutual, but polite, animosity.

Just then, Maude looked in their direction and headed over.

"I'm sure there's no danger in leaving you two alone, but nevertheless . . . How are you Morgan?"

Morgan ignored the question and asked, "Did you know Dr. Frazier, Maude?"

"Of course. We were the best of friends. Such a tragedy. But with her speciality . . ."

"You think she was killed by one of her patients?"

"Well, I assume so. Do you know anything, Morgan?"

"Maude, we really should be going," Lance interrupted.

"We must do lunch, Morgan." Maude allowed herself to be ushered away.

"Any Halloween," Morgan said silently to the insincere invitation.

"Please come with me to give my condolences to the family, Morgan." Victoria had rejoined her and was pulling on her arm. A small group was gathered around Mr. Frazier. The son stood alone, looking despondent. His suit must have been left over from high school graduation, Morgan thought as she noticed his wrists dangling below the cuffs and his trousers, which were too short, exposing red-and-green argyle socks.

"I'm so sorry about your mother," Victoria began as they joined the boy. "This is Morgan McRain, and I'm Victoria Trimbell. I shared an office suite with Lucinda." The boy didn't respond, so Victoria rattled on. "Of course, she was such a wonderful person. So many people will miss her."

"Not me," the young man said flatly. "She got what she deserved."

"Now, I know you don't really mean that, although it's healthy for you to express your anger," Victoria counseled. "Here's one of my business cards. Feel free to come see me."

The boy pocketed the card without looking at it and said, "I know where your office is."

"You must have visited your mother there lots of times," Morgan said.

"No. Just once."

"Was it the day she was killed?" Morgan couldn't help herself.

"Randolph has a strange sense of humor," said Mr. Frazier, breaking away from the small knot of people to join them. "You must be Victoria. Lucinda spoke so highly of you." Everyone shook hands, and Morgan introduced herself. Randolph wandered away.

"Terrible, terrible tragedy. We were separated, but we remained good friends. And of course, this is so hard on Randolph."

"He seems very angry with his mother," Morgan stated.

"Well, yes he is. You have to understand," Mr. Frazier looked at her with lively gray eyes. "Lucinda wasn't a naturally maternal person, and she viewed child rearing as an experiment. First, there was the Skinner box, and then, well, I don't think I need to go into all that now. It's enough to say that she and Randolph have always had a stormy relationship. But the boy will be fine. He's a sophomore at Stanford this year."

"Do you think he was angry enough to . . . ," Morgan started.

"Kill his own mother? Really, Dr. McRain, that's going a bit far! Besides, I was visiting him in Palo Alto the day Lucinda was murdered. If you will excuse me," Mr. Frazier moved away to greet other mourners.

"Morgan, I'm not sure you should get involved. Leave it to the police. You didn't even know Lucinda."

"From what I've heard so far, I think it's just as well. And to think she was friends with Maude Ross! Lucinda must have been an idiot. I can see one thing they had in common, though. Maude's raising her son as an experiment, too. I hope she got a good look at Randolph."

"Hello. Dr. McRain? This is Sam Reynolds. Detective Reynolds. We met in Lucinda Frazier's office the other day."

"Er, uh, do you wear glasses?"

"Yes. Yes, I do. I was wondering if you could meet me for lunch tomorrow, say about 12:30?"

"Just let me check my schedule," Morgan grabbed her appointment book and scanned the page for Thursday. "No, but I can make one o'clock if we meet close to my office. I'm downtown at Fifth and Yamhill. We could meet at Luigi's. It's in the same block."

"You got it." The line went dead before Morgan could ask, "Is this business or personal?"

※ ※ ※

"I have a hot lunch date tomorrow, April," she teased when they had settled in bed that night.

"Victoria?"

"No. Detective Reynolds."

"Be sure to bring him home to meet the family," April blandly responded, nuzzling the back of Morgan's neck.

* * *

Morgan's 12 o'clock appointment ran over slightly, and she had to hurry to Luigi's. She hoped she would recognize Detective Reynolds. She remembered that he wore glasses but little else about him.

She opened the restaurant door and surveyed the tables. He was in the corner booth, looking over the menu. A well-built man, he wore a tweed jacket, a gray button-down shirt, and a red tie, which was slightly askew.

"Hello, Detective," Morgan said as she slid across red Naugahyde opposite him.

"Sam," he corrected. "I'm glad to see you. I didn't realize they had Mexican food in this place. I expected Italian."

"Fools everybody, but it's good. I'm going to have the cheese enchiladas, hold the sour cream," she said to the waiter, who arrived just behind her.

"Beef and bean burrito smothered in guacamole, and we'll need more chips," Sam ordered. "Saw you at the funeral yesterday. I know you didn't see me. I heard you practically accuse young Frazier of murdering his mother."

Morgan looked up from the basket of tortilla chips to see if he was smiling. He wasn't. She decided to wait him out and not respond, check out the climate a little further. After all, she knew discovering the body made her a prime suspect.

"Where were you Monday morning between eight and ten?" His green eyes steadily held hers.

"Fortunately, that's easy to answer." Morgan took a long drink from her water glass to keep him waiting and to deliberately gain some sense of control. "I had clients at eight, nine, and ten. Of course, I do work fifty-minute hours. So I suppose I could have sprinted the half mile or so to Lucinda's office, strangled her, and run back to be on time for my next appointment. It was a little hard getting those panty hose off of her, though. And naturally I would arrange to do it on a day when I was having lunch with Victoria so I could be the one to find the body. And since I had never met the woman, my only motive

must be that I want to get rid of all the private practice therapists in town to dispose of the competition. I wonder who will
be next?"

Now he was smiling. "Just routine. You're not a suspect.
And in answer to your next question," a slight blush crawled up
his face, "I just thought lunch would be nice. I've never really
known a psychologist before."

"I've never really known an officer of the law before, and
now that I know dessert won't be handcuffs, I think lunch will
be nice, too." *Tell him,* a loud voice in Morgan's head instructed.
"Just for the record, you should know that I am ... involved."

"Life is complicated," Sam smiled and dug into the food
that had just arrived.

"Tell me, Sam, are you making any progress on the case?"
Morgan asked, when she finally had control of the cheese
dangling from her fork to the plate.

"Oh, we're checking out a lot of things. As you know, the
husband and son have alibis. We haven't turned up any real
enemies." Sam's voice was neutral.

"What about fingerprints, hairs, clothing fibers, semen?"
Morgan was curious besides feeling involved in the case.

"Did you read Nancy Drew books?" Sam laughed.

"Yes, and you must have had sisters, since you know Nancy
Drew," Morgan laughed back, enjoying herself. Maybe a friendship was possible. "Well?"

"Sure, there were fingerprints. Too many fingerprints. Dr.
Frazier's, the cleaning woman's, and umpteen sets that probably
belong to patients. The physical evidence isn't all that useful as
yet. And I can't tell you whether or not she was sexually
assaulted. We're withholding that information from the public."

"Why?"

"Partly to sort out the real murderer from the phonies."
Sam polished off his burrito. "We've already had two confes-
sions."

"And?" Morgan looked expectant.

Sam shook his head. "Well-known crazies. Neither of them
could have done it." He looked away for a minute before
directing his gaze at Morgan. "Actually, you could help me out."

Was somebody going to recognize her up-to-now hidden talent for sleuthing? "What do you have in mind?"

"We've interviewed all of her patients, and I'd like you to see one of them. He's really broken up about her death, and I can't make heads or tails out of him."

"Why not Victoria? She's the grief counselor."

"He won't go anywhere near the office. Will you do it? It would have to be gratis, of course. The department doesn't have a budget for this kind of thing. We'd consider you a volunteer consultant to the case."

"I'll see him once and assess his need for continued psychotherapy," Morgan became more formal. "Is this the real reason why you asked me to lunch?"

"Yes. And to see if you had ferreted out the guilty party yet."

"Where were you between eight and ten Monday morning, Detective Reynolds?"

5

"Please come in and have a seat." Morgan motioned to the scared-looking young man in her waiting room. He walked slowly into her office and then couldn't seem to decide whether to sit on the plaid sofa or in one of the matching easy chairs. He looked at each and then looked back at Morgan.

"Please, anywhere you like will be fine." Morgan tried to be reassuring. The man moved from one piece of furniture to another but still didn't sit. With what she hoped wasn't an audible sigh, Morgan sat in one of the chairs and pointed to the other.

"Sit there," she ordered. He seemed very relieved as he folded himself into the chair. With a practiced eye, Morgan assessed the man across from her. He appeared to be in his early twenties, slightly taller than average, thin, with a pale complexion and dark brown hair. He seemed to have dressed carefully. His hair was neatly combed, his shirt crisply pressed, and his worn shoes highly polished.

"David, Detective Reynolds said that you wanted to talk to me about Dr. Frazier's death. It must be hard for you to see someone new."

David nodded his head but remained silent.

"I imagine it was hard for you the first time you went to see Dr. Frazier." Morgan looked at him questioningly.

Several minutes went by, and just when Morgan thought she was going to have to try a new approach, David said, "Er, er, . . . yes."

"Can you tell me about it, David?"

"I, I, I don't know."

"Okay, that's fine. Let's start then with you telling me why you wanted to talk to me."

"He said I should."

"'He' being Detective Reynolds?"

David nodded.

"Why do you think he thought you should?"

"I guess because I don't know if . . . I can't talk about it!" David looked miserable.

Morgan decided to shift gears. "You can, and you will. Begin now," she ordered.

"Yes, ma'am. Should I tell you everything?" David was now eager to please, and Morgan only gave him a stern look. "I started seeing Dr. Frazier about six months ago because I have some problems . . . sexual problems, and she's been helping me. I still do the same stuff, but I don't feel so bad about it. Dr. Frazier said that was real progress. I guess I should tell you what I do," David looked beseechingly at Morgan.

"Look, David, I don't know if we're going to keep seeing each other or not. As I told you on the phone, I need to understand the nature of your problem to know whether I can help you or if it would be best for me to refer you to someone else. So tell me whatever you think I should know." Morgan liked to be as straightforward as possible with clients.

"You're not going to order me to tell you?" David seemed disappointed.

"Would Dr. Frazier have ordered you?" Morgan asked.

"Oh yes! She knew what I liked! I'm really going to miss her." David's eyes started to tear up.

"I'm sure you do miss her, David. It's okay to cry."

David blew his nose loudly into a wad of tissues. "That's what she always said, too. I'm okay. It's just . . . I think I may have killed her."

"You're not sure?" Morgan wondered how quickly she could beat it out the door. However, her more professional self dominated. "Maybe you had better tell me the whole story."

"I . . . I have trouble getting off, except when I masturbate," David was looking at the floor. "And there's more. I need to be wearing some article of women's clothing. And I like to be dominated by women. I dream of finding a dominatrix and being her sexual slave." David no longer seemed so shy. His eyes were shining, and his voice sounded gleeful.

"And Dr. Frazier was helping you to feel okay about these urges?"

"Yes." He looked up to meet Morgan's eyes. "And it was working. She would even give me orders. She wouldn't do anything sexual with me or anything like that, though. But she did say that my sexual dreams about her were okay."

"Did you feel okay about them?"

"Yeah." David legs bounced up and down. His fingers danced on the arms of the chair. "I did until they started getting violent. In my dreams, she would do all kinds of sexual things to me. And then the dreams flipped, and I started doing all kinds of sexual things to her. And the things got more and more violent. Finally, I started dreaming of killing her. Like in snuff movies." David seemed genuinely upset now.

"But these were only dreams, David."

"I hope so, but I'm not sure. Sometimes they would seem so real, and I'd wake up in a panic."

"When was the last time you saw Dr. Frazier?"

"I was supposed to see her the morning she died, but I overslept and missed my appointment. Or at least I think I did. I was having one of those dreams where I raped her and killed her. It was so real!" David paused and looked at Morgan. "Do you think I did it?"

6

"Morgan? Earth to Morgan? Where are you?"

"What? Oh, sorry, April. I was a million miles away." April and Morgan were gliding around Lloyd Center ice-skating rink hand in hand on Saturday morning. For the last few minutes April had been maneuvering Morgan safely around the other skaters she seemed determined to plow into.

"Let's sit down for a few minutes, Morgan." They made their way off the ice to the refreshment area.

"If I can trust you to stay put at this table and not cause bodily harm to anyone, I'll go get us some hot chocolate," April said. As she wobbled away, Morgan looked through the crowd of skaters, trying to pick out Donald and Priss. She looked for the matching red-and-green striped sweaters Donald had knitted, with long stocking caps to match. She spotted them in a corner, practicing figure eights. Donald was an excellent skater, and Priss already seemed to have grace and natural athletic ability. Morgan was just a little envious as she tried to tune out her own aching ankles.

"Here we go." April returned with two steaming white mugs of chocolate with candy cane stir-sticks. "Now, how about telling me what's keeping you from being here and enjoying this marvelous day?"

Morgan looked up and saw roses in April's cheeks and realized that indeed she had been oblivious to the day, the activity, and her companion. "I'm sorry. I just can't stop thinking about one of my clients."

April stopped slurping her drink long enough to say, "This is not like you, Morgan. Usually, you're really good at compartmentalizing your life." April's blue-green eyes registered concern.

Morgan took a napkin and reached over and wiped off April's chocolate mustache. "You're right. I usually don't think about my clients except when I'm with them. But I'm in a quandary as to how to proceed with the young man Detective Reynolds asked me to see."

"Go ahead and spill. I'll be your sounding board." April squeezed Morgan's hand.

"It probably will help to talk out loud. Goddess! I've been upside down, backwards, and sideways in my head," Morgan began. "It's possible this client murdered Lucinda Frazier. I don't know. I don't know him well enough to be certain what he's capable of or even how grounded in reality he is. And because of client confidentiality, I can't say anything to Sam."

"Sam?" April's eyebrows shot up toward her hairline.

"Detective Reynolds. His first name is Sam. He asked me to call him that."

"I see. Or maybe I don't, but I'll try to stay on topic here. This isn't my area of law, but I thought that in the case of homicide, your obligation to report to the authorities supersedes your client confidentiality."

"That's only if the client is threatening to murder somebody, not if he already has." Morgan wiped at her own chocolate mustache. "Also, this guy had a heavy-duty transference going with Lucinda, and I don't work with that model. I'm not sure I'm the best therapist for him, but maybe I'm just being chicken."

"If you think he might have killed his last therapist, I'd be really relieved if you'd refer him to someone else. Preferably someone you don't like."

Morgan gave April a "look."

"Mommy! Seymore!" When Priss was first learning to talk, April had frequently told her daughter to "see Morgan." Priscilla had translated this command into a nickname, which had stuck. "Come watch me skate!" Priss was running to them on her skates. "Wow! Hot chocolate! My tummy's cold."

"Do you think you can sit still long enough to drink some?" Morgan asked her favorite little girl.

"I don't think so." Priss looked very serious.

※ ※ ※

"Hi, Vic, this is Morgan. Got a minute?"

"Sure, Morgan, if you don't mind some background noise. I just gave Tuna Breath a bath, and I'm using the hair dryer on him."

"Don't you have to use two hands? One to hold him down?"

"Oh no, he loves it. Can't you hear him purr?" Victoria switched off the dryer for a moment and held the receiver to the feline. Loud, contented noises came through the phone. "I'm planning on bringing my date home tonight, and I want him to look his best."

"Who is it this time?"

"My hairdresser, Wynona. You know how it is when you've known someone for a long time and suddenly you see her in a whole new light? I was just having my hair trimmed the other day, and I looked in the mirror, and I saw these gorgeous brown eyes looking back at me. Anyway, what's up, Morgan?"

"I need to ask you about a client. Detective Reynolds who's investigating Lucinda Frazier's murder . . ."

"Is he the cute one with glasses?" Victoria interrupted.

"Yes. He asked me to see one of her clients. I did, and now I need to refer him on. Any ideas?"

"Well, I guess he could see Darrell Richardson. After all, he was supervising Lucinda with her so-called sexual perversity cases. He's been working in that area longer. He's probably even familiar with the case."

"Good idea. Do you know the guy, Vic? I just know that he's married to Corky Vanderpelt, a former client of his."

"And that they never slept together before marriage. I think we heard the same gossip. No, I don't really know him, either. I just know that Lucinda believed he was an excellent supervisor. You know, Portland's really not that big, but the mental health community is huge."

"I know. Everyone wants to live in the great Northwest. I can't blame them. I used to wish I was born someplace else so I could move here. Do the police know about Richardson's relationship to Lucinda, Vic?"

"I doubt it. It never occurred to me to mention it. Do you think it's relevant?"

"Who knows? But I'll probably mention it to Sa . . . , er, Detective Reynolds."

"Are you two keeping in touch?" Victoria's voice was teasing.

"Keep your mind on Tuna Breath, Vic."

17

"Thanks for meeting me here, Morgan," Sam said. They were lunching at Lenny's Deli. "I thought I'd introduce you to my favorite restaurant. I recommend the matzo ball soup. And the potato latkes are to die for." Sam exaggerated a Yiddish accent.

As usual, Morgan had rushed to be on time, so it was only now as she was settling into the overstuffed booth that the aromas of the place caught up with her. Onions, cabbage, fish. "Hmmmm. Smells wonderful. I'm impressed already."

A waiter who appeared to be in his late sixties approached the table. "Usual, Sammy?" Without waiting for a reply, he turned to Morgan. "Make it two, young lady?"

"Sure. Why not?" Morgan hoped that beef tripe wasn't among her companion's favorite dishes.

"Sammy!" A large, older woman pressed Sam's face into her impressive bosom.

"Aunt Adele, I want you to meet my friend, Morgan McRain," Sam managed when he had sufficiently disengaged himself.

"Oh, she's a looker, Sammy. Has your Ma seen her yet? Ida, come out of the kitchen and see Sammy's new girl!" The last line was bellowed across the room, and it seemed to Morgan that everyone in the restaurant was staring at her. She focused on Sam, who seemed to be enjoying himself.

Aunt Adele's identical twin sister, Ida, made her way to the table. She was wearing a huge white apron and tall chef's hat and had a wooden spoon in one hand and a whisk in the other. She leaned a cheek to Sam, waiting to be kissed. He obliged. "So you have a new girl, Sammy. What would it hurt to warn us? I could have made something special."

"All of your dishes are special, Ma. This is my friend," he said, emphasizing the word friend. "Morgan McRain. She's helping me with one of my cases."

"I'm pleased to meet you," said Morgan. "Is it Mrs. Reynolds? This is a wonderful place."

"Wait 'til you eat. Then tell me it's wonderful. I have to get back. You should call me tonight, Sammy, and I'll tell you what I think of your friend." She winked at Morgan as she left.

Adele brought them two bowls of thick borscht and two bottles of Dr. Brown's celery tonic. Morgan and Sam were alone again. "Samuel Leopold Reynolds, in case you're wondering. My father was Italian Catholic."

"So he wasn't Lenny?"

"No, that was Ma's father. He started this place forty years ago. I think all the waiters are originals. How do you like the borscht?"

"It's terrific. But why are we meeting like this?" Morgan thought it was time for some clarity.

"Besides liking your company, I thought you might have something to tell me after your interview with David." The waiter was back to set down steaming plates of cabbage rolls.

"This is very awkward. I can't really discuss David with you."

"Don't give me the details, especially not over lunch. Just tell me whether or not I should take him seriously as a suspect."

Morgan hesitated.s "I truly don't know," she said slowly. "Can anyone say where he was at the time of Lucinda's murder?"

"His father thinks he was in bed asleep, but he doesn't know for sure. The coroner has set the time of death at between eight and ten in the morning. David's father left the house at 9:30, and he thought David was in his room, but he never checked."

"I can't tell you anything more. I'm just not sure," Morgan reiterated. "I do have another piece of information for you. I just found out that Dr. Darrell Richardson, a psychiatrist in town, was Lucinda's supervisor. He might know if any of her clients were potentially dangerous."

"Good lead." Sam pulled out a small notebook and made a note.

"Now, you tell me something new about the case," Morgan demanded between the last bites of her cabbage roll.

"Actually, I will." Sam signaled to the waiter, "Two coffees, Herb." To Morgan he said, "We have a bit of a break in the case. We got an anonymous call saying that Randolph Frazier was really in town the night before the murder, not at Stanford visiting with his father as he claimed."

The coffees arrived, and plates were swept away. The waiter returned with two servings of cheesecake. "Now this is to die for," Morgan said after the first bite. "What are you going to do with this new information?"

"I interviewed Charlie Frazier again this morning, and he admitted he'd been lying. He says he was really in San Francisco on business."

"Can that be verified?"

"I like how your mind works, lady. I've got someone checking on that now."

"But why did he lie?"

"He says to protect the boy. He guessed that Randolph might be a suspect, and he wanted to provide him with an alibi."

"Wow! So, maybe I was right. If I had just kept at Randolph, he might have confessed at the funeral," Morgan lamented.

"Slow down, Sherlock. We don't know if he's really guilty or not. Besides, I'm going to give you another chance."

"What do you mean?"

"I'm going from here to interview Randolph again, and I want you to come with me."

"You do?" Morgan was genuinely surprised. "Why?"

"Because I think you make the boy pretty uncomfortable, and I think that'll be to my advantage."

"Okay. I'm free this afternoon." Morgan ran her hand through her hair. "And I must admit, I'm curious. But before we leave, Sam, what will you say to your mother tonight when you call her?"

"Nothing."

"Nothing?"

"Nothing. It's what she'll say to me you should worry about. She won't even give me a chance to talk."

"Sam?"

"Yes, Morgan?"

"I think you should meet my family. How about dinner Wednesday?"

8

Sam stopped his unmarked car in front of one of the large Tudor houses in the Alameda neighborhood. Until recently Lucinda Frazier had lived here. Morgan and Sam went up the curved walkway and rang the bell. Morgan had the impression that someone was peering at them from the peephole in the door, and then she heard footsteps running away from the door.

"Stay here!" Sam ordered as he leaped over the porch railing and ran to the back of the house.

"Oh great," Morgan thought to herself. "What if he comes charging through the door? What am I supposed to do? Bang him over the head with my handbag?" Soon there were sounds of scuffling and some shouting before everything was quiet again.

Morgan was still deciding between keeping to her assigned post or checking the back to make sure Sam was okay when the front door opened. Sam stood there with Randolph, both of them looking a little disheveled. Randolph looked more disheveled than Sam.

He was wearing flannel pajama bottoms and a long johns top, even though it was the middle of the afternoon. His copper-red hair was uncombed, and its scruffiness comple-mented the red stubble on his chin.

"Come on in, Morgan," said Sam. "Randolph says he prefers to talk to us here rather than at the station."

"Now then, Randolph, suppose you tell us where you were the morning your mother was killed," Sam spoke gruffly to the boy when they were seated in the yellow-and-blue living room.

"We've already been over this," Randolph whined. "I told you, my father was visiting me on campus."

"Cut the crap, kid!" Sam's voice held a threatening chill. "Your dad has admitted he wasn't in Palo Alto, and I hate being lied to!"

Randolph's already pale complexion turned paler, and Morgan thought she could see his blue eyes scrambling. "Dad told you he wasn't in Palo Alto? I don't believe it," he said without conviction.

"You better stop stalling and start talking fast, or it's your ass, kid. Why'd you lie?" Sam pressed.

"I, I . . . I wanted to give my Dad an alibi. I'm afraid he killed her," Randolph's voice was small. "I don't blame him if he did. She was a royal bitch."

"But why would he?" Sam asked.

"She was trying to take him for all he's worth in the divorce settlement, and she's got plenty of her own money. Look around, for Christ's sake!" Morgan looked. Her eye fell on a pair of Chinese porcelains on the mantel. It was probably true. Lucinda didn't seem to be hurting for bucks.

"Did your father ever threaten your mother?" Sam was not distracted.

"Are you kidding! It was the other way around. She was always saying things like she was going to hang him by the balls. I think she hated him. I think she hated all men!" Randolph glared at Morgan. "And I hated her."

"Which brings me back to my original question, where were you the morning your mother was killed?"

Randolph hung his head and didn't answer.

"I'm waiting," Sam reminded him.

"I have to think about it," Randolph said quietly.

"Look, punk, there's nothing to think about. You tell me the truth about where you were right now, or I'm taking you down to the station." Randolph remained silent. "Okay, have it your way, pal." Sam pulled a pair of handcuffs out of a leather pouch that was attached to his belt.

"I want to talk to a lawyer." Randolph was beginning to cry.

"Okay. Use the phone, and have one meet us at the station." The boy picked up the phone book, and Morgan wondered if he were going to choose legal counsel from the yellow pages. Sam came over to her and whispered quietly in her ear, "I'm putting the kid on. While we're doing this, why don't you have a look upstairs in her room? I think you'll find it interesting."

Morgan nodded. She climbed the broad, carpeted stairs and entered what she assumed to be the owner's suite. The door to a large dressing room stood open. There was a long row of leather outfits and military costumes of all sorts and another of lacy black things. A collection of whips was displayed along one wall. Morgan considered trying on a silk teddy with holes cut out for the nipples but decided against it. And then she had a fantasy of descending the stairs in a police chief's uniform and watching Sam's face. She thought about the sedate blue suit Lucinda was buried in and shook her head.

2

"What's come over you, Morgan? Rummaging through a dead woman's closet!" April was aghast that evening as Morgan recounted the day's events. "You've been acting weird ever since you got involved with this investigation."

"I don't know. I was curious."

"So, did Sam actually arrest Randolph?" April wanted to know.

"No. He never intended to, really. It was all a bluff." Morgan took a sip of peppermint tea and ran her fingers through her hair. They were sitting at the kitchen table. "Poor kid. He called about ten lawyers from the yellow pages, who were all in meetings, out of the office, or wanted a huge retainer."

"I'm glad he didn't call me," April poured more tea from a cabbage-shaped pot with a carrot for the handle.

"Me, too. He finally gave up and told Sam he'd been with his girlfriend the morning his mother was killed. He'd spent the night at her house."

"Why the big secret?" April asked while munching an almond cookie.

"Because he'd sneaked in her window. She still lives at

home with her mother." Morgan reached over and took a bite of April's cookie. "It's kind of sweet when you think he was willing to go to jail to keep her from getting in trouble with her mom. And guess who her mom is?"

"Dr. Joyce Brothers."

"Close." Morgan grabbed a cookie just as April was firmly putting the lid on the jar. "Ashton Wilder, my grad school friend!"

"Randolph is dating Clarissa? She wears a black-and-silver mohawk, and she's afraid to let her mother know she's sexually active?"

"I don't think Clarissa is as tough as she looks. She's only sixteen." Morgan pushed back from the table and ran her hand through her unruly curls again. "At any rate, assuming Clarissa backs him up, I guess Randolph is off the hook."

"Unless they're both lying. He could probably talk her into covering up for him." April patted her own hair, which was still damp from the shower. She was wearing yellow flannel jammies complete with feet. "So what are you two detectives going to pursue next?"

"Actually, we have an appointment tomorrow morning to interview Darrell Richardson. He's been Lucinda's supervisor, so he may have some leads, and I also want to refer that client I told you about to him."

April took Morgan's hand, "I'm relieved, honey."

Priss and Donald bounded in through the back door. "Mommy! Seymore! The wicked witch made Snow White eat an apple. It was rotten and she died but this man kissed her and she wasn't dead anymore and the dwarfs were happy. So were the birds!"

Morgan, April, and Donald had had several discussions about Walt Disney. Both April and Donald maintained that the movies were an important part of the American folk culture, and they didn't want to deprive Priss. Morgan could remember hiding under the seat during Snow White when she was three and thought that twelve might be an appropriate age for such exposure. She had lost. "Were you scared?" she asked Priss, helping her out of her coat, scarf, and mittens.

"Uh-huh," Priss solemnly nodded her head. "When can I go again?"

※ ※ ※

Darrell Richardson was a placid-looking man with neatly trimmed blonde hair, a small mustache, and big, even teeth in an Eleanor Roosevelt mouth. Although he looked quite fit, Morgan couldn't imagine him working out in a gym. He didn't seem the type. Too dignified to sweat.

"Of course, I would be happy to take over David's treatment," he was saying to Morgan.

"From what you've learned in your supervision sessions with Dr. Frazier, do you think David could have killed her?" Sam asked the psychiatrist bluntly.

"I couldn't possibly offer a professional opinion, Detective. I've yet to meet the young man. I'm certain Dr. McRain could answer that query better than I." He looked directly at Morgan. "What is your professional opinion?"

Morgan wasn't sure why this middle-aged man made her feel so squirmy. "I've already given it to the detective," she hedged.

"Please enlighten me," Dr. Richardson insisted.

"I don't know," Morgan said flatly.

"In terms of the other clients Dr. Frazier discussed with you," Sam carried on, "are there any that we should be looking at more closely?"

"In spite of what I just said about not giving a professional opinion as to whether or not David is capable of murder, in more general terms, I believe each of us is capable of violence if the right circumstances present themselves. I simply don't know if the circumstances were right for any of the people Lucinda had been seeing. But, Detective Reynolds, I wouldn't rule any of them out." Dr. Richardson stood up with an air of dismissal. "If I can be of any further assistance, please don't hesitate to contact my secretary. Pleasure to meet you, Dr. McRain." He extended his hand, and Morgan found herself holding limp fingers.

※ ※ ※

April and Priss were in the kitchen, by prior arrangement, helping Donald with dinner when the doorbell rang Wednesday evening. April was fine with meeting Sam; she just wanted Morgan to set him straight first.

Morgan took Sam's coat and a bouquet of freesias from him. They sat in chairs by the fire sipping glasses of sparkling cranberry juice. Morgan finally began, "I've really enjoyed getting to know you over the past few days, Sam." She took a deep breath, "That's why I wanted you to meet my family." Sam smiled and she hurried on, "There's April, my lover, and her daughter, Priss. And April's brother, Donald, lives with us. And . . . " Morgan was out of breath, so she stopped.

"I'm looking forward to meeting them," Sam didn't miss a beat. He looked around. "Where's everyone hiding?"

"I'll be right back." Morgan went into the kitchen, giving April the high sign and a kiss on the cheek for good measure. April took Morgan's hand, and they all returned to the living room.

After introductions, everyone drank cranberry juice and talked about the weather, the house, recent movies, and the police bureau. When Donald excused himself to check on dinner, Sam insisted on helping.

As the swinging door to the kitchen closed, April said, "He seems very nice, and he is cute. How'd he take the news?"

"I'm not sure it was news to him." Morgan realized she felt a little off center.

"Can men be cute?" Priss wanted to know.

"Yes, sweetie. Anyone can be cute," Morgan answered. "But especially you!" She took hold of the child's cheek and squeezed gently. "Let's see what the guys are doing." After they were seated at the big oak table and the dishes were being passed, Sam sniffed deeply at the cassoulet. "This smells heavenly."

"It has piggies' feet in it!" Priss announced. "Why don't we eat cows' feet?"

"I don't know," said April. "Aren't they made into glue?"

"Isn't that horses' hooves?" Donald asked.

"I ate chicken feet and ducky feet!" Priss declared.

"Dim sum," Morgan and April laughingly said together to explain to Sam. After apricot mousse, Donald, Morgan, and Sam settled into the living room with decaf. April took Priss upstairs to bathe her and put her to bed.

Morgan stretched out on the sofa. She realized that she had been slightly tense all evening and was more comfortable with Sam when April wasn't around. She had been feeling that somehow she had to protect each of them from the other. Silly. Actually, they had seemed quite at ease.

"Tell me what's new in the murder investigation," Donald said to Sam.

"Mostly a lot of dead ends. Both Randolph's and Mr. Frazier's new alibis checked out."

"Someone verified that Charlie was in San Francisco?" Morgan asked.

"Yeah, one of his business associates."

"Did any of Lucinda's clients have a shoe fetish?" Morgan asked.

"Huh?" Sam was nonplussed by the subject change.

"I just remembered again about her missing shoes," Morgan said. "Lucinda Frazier was barefoot, and I didn't see her shoes lying around anywhere."

"Well, naturally they had to come off in order to get at the panty hose. But you're right, I don't think we found them. You could be on to something. Why didn't you mention this sooner?"

"I did," Morgan pouted. "That first day, but you weren't interested, and then I forgot about them. I think Donald reminded me just now." Both Sam and Morgan looked at Donald, who was sitting on the sofa in a very handsome brown-and-gray kimono. He had kicked off his black house-boy slippers and was barefoot.

"I'm glad I could be such an inspiration." Donald winked at Sam.

"I'll have someone go back over Dr. Frazier's client files and look for mention of fetishes. Do you think a foot fetish and a shoe fetish are the same thing?" Sam asked Morgan.

She shrugged her shoulders. "It depends. These things can be highly specialized, but since she was strangled with her panty hose, maybe we're looking for someone who goes for footwear of all kinds."

"Speaking of feet," Sam said to Donald, "I'd love to have your recipe for cassoulet."

10

It was a white, standard, business-size envelope. Morgan held it carefully by one corner with her right thumb and forefinger. It had arrived in the mail at her office along with the usual insurance checks, bills, and flyers for the latest post-traumatic stress syndrome and addictive organizations workshops.

What distinguished this particular envelope from all the rest was the fact that Morgan's name and address were spelled out with individual letters cut from a glossy magazine. Morgan hesitated momentarily before punching out the digits of Sam's number at Central Precinct with her left hand.

"Detective Perry speaking."

"Is Detective Reynolds available, please?" Morgan asked.

"Who wants to know?"

"This is Dr. Morgan McRain calling."

"Sam, it's that lady who found the dead shrink," Morgan heard the detective announce.

"Hi, Morgan. I was going to call you this morning, but you beat me to it." Morgan was relieved to hear Sam's voice. "That was a great dinner last night. I enjoyed meeting your family."

"Thanks, Sam. I had a good time, too. But look, that isn't why I called." Morgan was gripping the envelope so hard that her thumb was beginning to cramp. "Uh, actually, Sam, I was wondering how small bombs could be? I mean, in this age of computer chips and all, April has a watch that not only can tell time in any foreign capital, it can play the national anthem of every country and . . ."

"Morgan! Stop rambling and tell me what's up!" Sam commanded. Morgan stopped and took a deep breath.

"Sam, I just got an envelope in the mail that scares me. My name and address are in cut-out letters."

"Regular-size envelope?"

"Business-size. It's bigger than my personal stationery but the same as my professional stationery." Morgan felt beads of sweat lining up on her eyebrows. "Not as big as a manila envelope. Do you want me to measure it? I think I could probably borrow a ruler from the secretary in the next office."

"Open it."

"Are you sure, Sam?"

"It's too small for a bomb, computer chips notwithstanding. Go ahead and open it."

"Should I be careful about fingerprints?"

"Sure. There probably aren't any that don't belong to postal employees, but yeah, you might as well be careful."

Morgan stuck the telephone receiver between her shoulder and cheek and used her left hand to open her desk drawer and dig around among the paper clips, stick-em pads, pens that needed refills, and other equally useful things to locate her letter opener. She broke a fingernail in the process. "Ouch!"

"What's wrong?" Sam was quick to respond.

"Nothing. Just a minute." Morgan located the opener and still holding the envelope, carefully slid the blade under the gummed flap and pulled out the white paper inside. She unfolded it and found more cut-out letters.

"It says, 'Keep your big nose out of places it doesn't belong if you know what's good for you. Somebody close to you could get hurt.'" Morgan absently rested her chin on her right thumb and rubbed her forefinger up and down the side of her nose.

"Anything else?"

"No."

"Anything distinctive about the paper? Can you see a water-mark?"

"No. It looks ordinary, like something from the five and dime."

"Probably is. Okay, I'll be there in ten minutes to pick it up. Won't hurt to run it through the lab."

"Sam?"

"Yes?"

"Do you think my nose is big?"

11

Morgan walked up the brick path to the porch bordered by camellia bushes. She pushed the doorbell of the white bungalow and listened to the *1812 Overture*. Victoria opened the door and enthusiastically greeted her in a brilliantly colored spandex running outfit.

"Morgan! This is great. Now I have an excuse not to go for a run. I really didn't want to, but I polished off a banana-cream pie earlier, and I wanted to look my best for a date tonight, and well, anyway, come in."

Morgan walked through the entrance hall to the living room, which was dominated by Victoria's passion: early Alaskan folk art and religious symbols. Huge masks of birdlike faces covered the walls of the room. A small dugout canoe was suspended on the wall above the sofa, and a short totem pole stood beside the fireplace.

As soon as Morgan settled into one of the gray chairs, thirty pounds of fur landed in her lap. "Hello, Tuna Breath," she said. Morgan wasn't really a cat person. In fact, she was quite allergic, but Victoria was the love-me-love-my-cat sort, and after all, this was her house. Grimacing inwardly, she tried to shift the weight slightly and make the best of it. She was rewarded by loud, rasping purrs.

"He's always liked you! He's very particular, you know. He can sense when people like him."

"I'm sure he can." Morgan tried to ignore the claws kneading the flesh of her thighs. "I stopped by, Vic, because I'm feeling a little shaky." Morgan told her about the letter she'd received that morning.

"Gosh, this is just like an Agatha Christie whodunit! Please be really careful, Morgan. Seriously, I think you should drop the whole investigating thing. Or is it the detective you can't drop?"

"Actually, I had him to dinner last night so he could meet April, Priss, and Donald."

"How did that go over?"

"Terrific." She tried to adjust Tuna Breath again and received a warning stare.

"How has Sam responded to this change?"

"Very well. In fact, it's almost seemed too easy. I don't quite get it. But he seems to still like me." Morgan tentatively scratched Tuna Breath behind his ears. "Tell me about this hot date you have tonight."

"I'm not sure about the 'hot' part. But I met an interesting woman at breakfast at Cup and Saucer the other day. She asked me for my marmalade and then my phone number."

"What's she like?"

"Her name is Cynthia. She's a chemist and has the most amazing blue eyes."

"Goddess, Vic. I can see it coming. You'll be madly in love for two weeks, and then you'll discover she has weirdly shaped toenails, and you won't be able to see yourself being with someone with weird toenails, so you'll drop her and then feel guilty for the next three months." Morgan stopped scratching the cat's ear, and his tail began to swing from side to side. "What happened with Wynona?"

"Weird toenails. It's easy for you to be so sarcastic. Not everyone's found their April yet. Back to your poison-pen letter. You know, I've been feeling pretty uncomfortable in my office ever since Lucinda's demise. As a matter of fact, I called April at her office about an hour ago and asked her what she thought my chances were for getting out of my lease."

"What'd she say?"

"She thinks I have sufficient reason. She's going to write a letter to my landlord for me. Want an orange juice?"

"Sure." Morgan started to rise to follow Vic into the kitchen, but Tuna Breath gave her a warning growl. Well, more of a hiss, really.

"Stay put. I'll only be a minute." At the sound of the refrigerator door opening, Tuna Breath lunged from Morgan's lap, puncturing her thighs in the process. A moment later, Morgan heard a blood-curdling scream from the kitchen. When Morgan got there, she saw Victoria bent over in front of the open refrigerator. Tuna Breath was on top of her with all twenty claws spread into Victoria's back. Before Morgan could react, Victoria flung herself over onto her back, forcing the feline to release her flesh. She lay on top of the cat a moment before getting up.

"Sorry I scared you," Vic said as she took Morgan's hand to pull herself up.

"Good Goddess! What got into him?"

"Oh, this is that routine I told you about. We go through it every morning when I'm getting his cat food out."

"Couldn't you put it on a higher shelf?"

"Yes, but that would spoil one of his few pleasures."

Victoria and Morgan returned to the living room with two large glasses of juice. Tuna Breath returned to Morgan's lap, where he immediately dunked his face into Morgan's glass. "Don't worry, he just had a bath. Oh, here, I know you're going to be squeamish," said Victoria. "Let's trade." They swapped glasses, and Morgan carefully held hers out of feline range.

"Have you thought about where you might relocate your office?"

"I've been asking around. There's a vacant space in the Taylor Building. You know, on Tenth Street. There are several therapists who're in the building already."

"That's where Darrell Richardson and Corky Vanderpelt have their offices."

"Yes. As a matter of fact, the vacancy is right next to their suite. I just called to talk to him about it. Lucinda really liked the guy. And he has this gem of a secretary, a Mrs. Hatfield, who would be available to me as well."

"How expensive?"

"Well, that's part of what's so appealing. He's offering it to me for only half of what I pay now, and currently the only secretary I have is a phone machine."

"Hmmmm. He didn't really seem like the type to extend himself like this."

"Oh, you're becoming really suspicious of people since you started this investigating stuff. I think the guy feels sorry for me because of Lucinda." Victoria finished her juice. "Or maybe he's a phony liberal who thinks having an Asian-Inuit, lesbian office mate would be cool." Morgan just shrugged her shoulders. "Well, I'm going to give the guy the benefit of the doubt. With the savings, we could start calling you Lobster Breath, eh, kitty?" With the mention of his favorite food, the cat gave a loud, plaintive meow, leaped from Morgan's lap, and roared to the kitchen.

12

"Morgan! Telephone!"

"Okay, Donald. I've got it." Morgan hrrumphed a few times to clear the sleep out of her voice before speaking into the receiver. "This is Morgan McRain."

"Good morning. Hope I didn't wake you." Sam's voice was cheery.

"Not at all." Morgan fought back a yawn. "What's up?"

"Unfortunately, nothing. No prints on the letter, of course. The paper is sold at half a dozen places in the area. But I thought if you were free for lunch we could review what we have so far. Sometimes it helps to point out another line of inquiry. Frankly, this case is going nowhere fast."

"Lunch is fine if you can make it at one. I've got a noon client. Where shall we meet?"

"How about some of that dim sum Priss mentioned the other night?"

"Okay. Let's meet at Fong Chong's on Fourth and NW Everett."

"Fong Chong's for dim sum it is. See ya."

Morgan pulled on a forest green robe, ran her fingers through her curls, and made her way downstairs to the kitchen.

She followed her nose to the coffee pot, poured a cup, and joined Donald and Priss at the breakfast table.

"Morning, Morgan," Donald said around a mouthful of yogurt, granola, and raisins.

"I'm being a baby today," Priss chirped. Morgan brought her eyes into focus and noticed that Priss had abandoned her spoon. She was using her fingers to separate the granola and raisins from her yogurt. There was a little pile of each on either side of her bowl.

Morgan gave Priss a kiss on the top of her head, which seemed to be the only clean part available. "Why didn't you just ask Uncle Donald to leave off the granola and raisins?"

"'Cause I like picking them out."

"Now why didn't I think of that?"

"Priss is being a baby now because this afternoon she's being a big girl and going to preschool," Donald explained.

Priss nodded solemnly. She had only recently begun attending preschool after much debate around the house. Finally, everyone had agreed on two afternoons a week. Donald, April, and Morgan had interviewed at several centers before choosing one where lesbian households were the norm.

"What's your favorite thing about preschool so far, honey?" Morgan asked as she took out a couple of slices of Italian herb bread from the toaster.

"Two things. I like the bunnies. Mr. Big Ears and Bunno. Mr. Big Ears is going to have babies, so I can't hold her, but I get to feed her carrots."

"Bunnies are nice. What's the second thing?" Morgan was spreading her toast with lemon curd.

"There are two bunnies. I like them both!"

"Oh. Do you like anything else?"

"Yeah. Finger paints!" Priss began drawing patterns on the table with her yogurt hands.

"Babies usually take morning naps," Donald reminded her. Priss reached for her spoon. "April's got an ACLU meeting tonight, and I've got a date. So you two are on your own for dinner."

"Anyone I know?"

"American Civil Liberties Union? I'm surprised you're not familiar with them, Morgan."

"Very funny."

※ ※ ※

Fong Chong's was crowded with formica-topped tables and black plastic chairs. The aisles were just wide enough to accommodate the stainless steel steam carts full of Chinese delicacies.

Morgan actually preferred the tamer rice noodles, pot stickers, and tuna cakes, but since this was Sam's first time, they'd also selected chicken and duck feet, paper-wrapped chicken, stuffed tofu, and of course, sticky rice.

"This stuff is great," Sam said, crunching a chicken's foot.

Morgan poured more jasmine tea. "So, no leads at all?"

"Well, obviously the killer knows you've been helping me. That's something. But let's take it from the top." Sam wiped his mouth with his already greasy napkin. "You discover Lucinda Frazier's half-nude body lying on the couch in her office at noontime. She'd been strangled with her own panty hose."

"You never did tell me whether or not she'd been sexually molested."

Sam glanced around before he said, "This is top secret. You have to promise not to tell anyone. Not even April or Donald." Morgan nodded. "Well, I don't know if molested is the right word or not. We know she had intercourse, but there was no sign of a struggle. And the guy used a condom. So he must have taken the time to put one on. Not typical for a rapist."

"You know he used a condom because there was no semen?"

"That, and this was a prelubricated condom. There was a residue in her . . . "

"So you found the condom?"

"No, but we've been able to identify three possible brands based on the lubricant sample: Sheik, Sensation, and Maxx.

"Never heard of them."

"And you're quite familiar with condoms?"

"No." Morgan blushed.

"Actually, they're common brands, so that doesn't really get us anywhere."

"So you're sure it was a man because of the intercourse and the condom." Morgan paused to point to and acquire a plate of custard tarts from a passing cart. "Have you considered the fact that a woman could use a condom on a dildo?"

Now it was Sam's turn to blush. "Actually, I thought I'd ask you about that. Is it a common practice?"

"Very." Morgan said. "After all, it's important to practice safer sex."

"Let's go on," Sam said, making a note. "After the sexual, uh, . . . experience, she was strangled with the panty hose."

"Could she have been strangled first?"

"I don't know. The coroner can't tell."

"What do we have next?" Morgan refilled their teacups. "Oh, I know. The missing shoes. Any luck with either the shoes or following up on that idea about foot fetishes?"

"I haven't gotten anywhere with the foot fetish thing yet. I'm thinking about talking to Dr. Richardson again and finding out what he knows on the subject." Sam started piling up all the little empty saucers on the table. "We had a piece of luck with the shoes, however. I went back and checked out all the footwear in her closet. It seems that Lucinda had rather odd feet. They were extremely narrow in the heel and broad in the toes. She had her shoes custom made."

"Have you located the cobbler?"

"I've got somebody working on it as we speak." Sam leaned back in his chair. "Now, for suspects we have David, Mr. Frazier, and Randolph." He ticked them off with his fingers. "Randolph and Frazier have good alibis, and I don't really think David is our man, although I should ask Richardson about him, too."

"We need some new suspects," Morgan said, propping her elbows on the table, lacing her fingers, and resting her chin on them.

"Ah, so. Let's go visit your esteemed colleague Darrell Richardson."

13

Sam and Morgan had no sooner strapped themselves into Sam's car when his cellular phone rang. "Reynolds here." Sam listened awhile before saying, "Full confession?" And a little later, "Be right there. "

He turned to Morgan, "Dr. Richardson will have to wait. Seems I was wrong. David just turned himself in. I'd like you to hear his confession. After all, you're the expert."

"Sure." Morgan grabbed at the tiny armrest as Sam raced through traffic. "But I'm shocked. I didn't really take David seriously as a suspect either."

"We'll all be taking him seriously now." Sam looked grim as he darted from lane to lane and barely made it through an "orange" light. In less than five minutes, they were walking into the detective headquarters on the ninth floor of Central Precinct.

Morgan recognized Burly hurrying up to them. "Got him down the hall. Phillips is babysitting him."

"Has he asked for a lawyer?"

"Naw. We could barely shut him up long enough to give him the Miranda. This kid is singin' his head off in between cryin' jags. He's a mess."

"Okay. I'll take over." Sam headed down a hallway, with Morgan at his heels. "You can watch from in here." Sam pulled open a door. Inside was a small room with a couple of chairs facing a one-way mirror. Morgan sat down and saw David sitting in a straight-backed chair right in front of her. He had his head in his hands and was sobbing loudly. Morgan felt like a voyeur.

There was also a young man with sandy-colored hair and a mustache in the room. Morgan assumed this was Phillips. Sam stuck his head in the door and motioned to Phillips, who followed him out. David didn't seem to notice and continued crying. Two minutes later, Sam came back into the dingy room alone.

"Hello, David." The young man looked up. Sam handed him a box of tissues. David wiped his eyes, blew his nose, and looked mournfully at the detective.

"I'm sorry I didn't tell you before. I didn't know for sure." Sam glanced at a large reel-to-reel tape recorder to make sure it was running. Morgan also noticed a wall-mounted video camera.

"How do you know for sure now?" he asked softly.

"Dr. Richardson helped me sort it out. I know I did it. It wasn't a dream. I'm so sorry." David shook with sobs. Morgan found herself looking away. She was very used to observing grief, but being behind this mirror made her feel indecent somehow.

Sam let the young man cry for a few minutes. Speaking gently he said, "David, I know you've told the other officers all about it, but I need for you to tell me, step by step, what happened. Will you do that?"

David nodded his head. "I woke up that morning, and I had been dreaming about her, about Dr. Frazier. Sexual dreams. I went in for my appointment, and I was telling her about my dreams. I took her hand and said 'I'll show you.' She didn't resist. I think she thought it was good for me to be the aggressor. But I didn't rape her or anything."

"What did you do, David?"

"I just put her hand on my crotch so she could feel my erection. She didn't pull it away. And I got so hard. So I held on to her hand and used it to unzip my pants. Then I led her to the couch. And she lay down. I pulled up her dress. She took her shoes and panty hose off. Can I have a glass of water?"

Sam went to the watercooler in the corner of the room, filled a paper cup and handed it to David, who was no longer crying but was very flushed. Morgan wished for a cup of water, too, but there was no machine in her cubicle, and she didn't think rapping on the glass was a good idea.

When David finished the water, he crumpled the paper cup and continued. "We just had intercourse like two normal people. I got a hard-on, I penetrated her, I came, she came. That was all. I felt really successful. I thought I was cured. Then I picked up the panty hose and strangled her to death."

"Why?"

"I don't know." David hung his head. "Dr. Richardson says maybe I can't handle success."

14

"This is the life!" April lowered herself into the backyard hot tub. Morgan stuck her right foot against a water jet and giggled as the pressure tickled her sole. After several minutes the restful silence was broken by Morgan sitting up so abruptly that she lost her balance and plunged bottom first under the water. Sputtering, she surfaced and regained her seat.

"April! I just thought of something! David didn't mention the condom!"

"What condom?"

Morgan raised herself up on the edge of the tub to cool off a bit. "The person who murdered Lucinda Frazier used a condom. The police have narrowed it to three brands: Sheik, Sensation, or Maxx. And David didn't mention using one at all in his confession."

"Whoa!" April joined Morgan on the edge of the tub, sitting across from her. "Just because he didn't mention putting on a condom doesn't mean he didn't do it, you know. Condoms are rarities in our life, but that doesn't mean they are in everyone else's. Especially a heterosexual male in his twenties. It's probably as commonplace to him as . . . "

"Unzipping his pants?"

"Yeah. Something like that."

"He mentioned unzipping his pants."

"You think he's innocent?"

"I know he's innocent, but this proves it." Morgan splashed her feet up and down in the water. "Not only that. I know who did it!"

"Who?"

"Dr. Darrell Richardson!"

"I'm not following." April returned to the water.

Morgan slid down beside her and said, "Well, first of all, David's statement didn't ring true. It was as though he had rehearsed it, over and over again. I think he had. I think he did exactly that with Richardson. He even said he wasn't sure he had done it until Richardson 'helped' him 'sort it out.' I think the psychiatrist was trying to save his own hide by convincing David that he did it!"

"Wait a sec, Morgan. Weren't you the one who referred David to Richardson in the first place?"

"Sure, but what does that have to do with anything?" Morgan stretched, and April plopped her feet into Morgan's lap.

"Well, just think about it. Richardson boffs Lucinda, strangles her for Goddess-knows-what reason, and just keeps a low profile until, luck-of-all-luck, you refer a young man to him who's been dreaming of killing her and thinks maybe he even did kill her. He talks this kid into making a confession! Doesn't that sound just a little too lucky to you?"

"W-e-e-l-l," Morgan said weakly. "I know it sounds a little far-fetched, but I still think I'm right."

"There's one way to find out," April rolled her eyes at Morgan. "Call up your friend Corky Vanderpelt and ask her what brand of condoms her husband uses."

"I don't really know her all that well, but maybe I could work it into a conversation somehow." Morgan pushed April's legs off and leaped out of the tub. She grabbed a thick, green towel and headed in the back door.

"Hey! I was only kidding!" April called.

Morgan was back in two minutes. "He wasn't home."

"Richardson?"

"No," Morgan laughed. "Sam." She started drying herself off. "Where's Donald tonight?"

"He had another date."

"With whom?"

"Darrell Richardson." April ducked as a green towel flew by.

15

Monday morning, on their way to interview Darrell Richardson, Morgan shared her theory with Sam. "Doesn't the fact that David didn't mention using a condom prove he's innocent?" Morgan asked after summarizing her conclusions.

"He didn't mention it, but when we booked him he had to empty his pockets and . . . "

"Let me guess, a real Sensation fell out."

"Close. It was a Maxx."

"But don't you think his confession sounded rehearsed?"

"That's the first thing I want to ask Richardson about."

Sam opened the door, and Morgan went first into the waiting room of the suite that served Darrell Richardson, M.D., and his wife, Dr. Corky Vanderpelt-Richardson, Licensed Psychologist. They approached Mrs. Hatfield's desk. The tiny woman with the helmet of iron gray curls recognized them from their previous visit. "Hello, Detective. Dr. McRain. May I help you?"

Sam responded, "We're here to see Dr. Richardson again."

"Dr. Richardson is with a client. Is there anything I can do to help? He won't be free for quite a while."

"It's important that we speak with him," Sam said.

"Oh, dear. Just let me see what I can do. Please make yourselves comfortable." She left the room through a doorway that led to the inner sanctum. Morgan and Sam sat side by side on a peach chintz love seat. Morgan thought they probably looked like they were here for couple's counseling. She picked up a *People* magazine to read about the latest Hilary Rodham Clinton put-down.

Two paragraphs into the story, Mrs. Hatfield returned, trailing Corky Vanderpelt, who was wearing a purple minidress and orange-red pumps that matched her hennaed hair. Corky was always a hit at psychological conventions.

"If you'll just come this way, Detective," Corky threw back her left arm, indicating the doorway. The gesture hiked up her skirt. "Hello, Morgan," she said as the two therapists passed each other, "It's good to see you." Corky led them to an office that was obviously her own. Red, orange, and pink floor pillows dotted a deep purple, plush carpet. There were no chairs. Corky ushered them in, closed the door, and plopped down on an orange pillow. Morgan pulled her eyes away from Corky's thighs to look at a bright pink, plastic telephone with a flashing red button. Corky ignored it.

"Please," she said, gesturing to the pillows. Morgan selected a red pillow and seated herself, immediately wondering if she was going to have to struggle to her feet again, as Sam remained standing.

"Actually, we're here to see Dr. Richardson," he said.

"My husband is in session just now. Maybe I can help."

"All right." Sam spread his legs apart, adjusted his weight evenly over each knee, and folded his arms across his chest. Morgan was glad he wasn't staring at her like that. "How well did you know Lucinda Frazier?"

"Dr. Frazier and I had a professional relationship, of course, and I knew my husband supervised her, but I didn't really know her socially," Corky responded.

"What kind of professional relationship did you have?" Sam pushed.

"Oh, I didn't really mean we had a relationship," Corky said quickly. "I just meant we were all colleagues in the same profession. I'm a sex therapist, and she specialized in sexual dysfunctions. So we'd see each other at professional meetings and things."

"And things?" Sam repeated.

"Just a figure of speech, Detective. I only saw her at professional meetings. Dr. McRain knows what those are like."

"I know what professional meetings are like," Morgan said neutrally. She didn't want her acquaintance with Corky to influence the investigation.

"You didn't know Lucinda socially at all?" Sam persisted.

Corky paused. She seemed to have an acute interest in her fingernails, examining each one in turn, before finally replying, "Just to chat if we ran into each other somewhere. That's all."

"What was she like as a person?" Morgan asked.

Corky smiled at her and said, "She took herself very seriously. She was probably a good therapist. I think she was very devoted to her work. More than she was to her family."

"What do you mean?" asked Sam.

"Her husband always looked a little neglected to me."

"Do you know Mr. Frazier?"

"No. Not really. I've just met him a few times." She looked at Sam and added, "At professional gatherings."

"Dr. Richardson," Sam began.

"That's Vanderpelt-Richardson," Corky corrected.

"Dr. Vanderpelt-Richardson." Sam's voice took on a deep, authoritative tone, which by now Morgan recognized went with his bluffing. "I'd like you to come down to the station this afternoon and take a polygraph."

"What?" Corky indignantly popped up off her pillow.

"That's right. I'll send a squad car for you at three."

"What?" Corky repeated herself.

"I don't think you're telling me the truth about your relationship with Lucinda Frazier, and there's a simple way to find out. The officers will pick you up at three. Allow at least four hours." Sam turned to the door. "Let's go, Morgan."

"Wait!" Corky sounded desperate. "Darrell's going to kill me, but I suppose someone should tell you."

"Tell me what?" Sam asked quietly.

Corky looked at Morgan. Morgan thought she was going to ask her to leave, but she sighed and said to Sam, "Lucinda was a swinger. She and her husband belonged to a club. They went even after they separated."

"She told you this?"

Corky's face was as red as her hair. "Darrell and I belong, too."

Morgan felt her eyes go round with surprise. She blinked and closed her mouth, which seemed to be open for no reason. She certainly had nothing to say. Even Sam was dumbstruck. Finally, he said, "Tell me more about this club."

"We call it the Chandelier Club, you know, like swinging from chandeliers. Anyway, there are five couples."

"I need the names," said Sam, pulling out a notebook and pen.

"Besides Darrell and me and Lucinda and Charlie, there's Norma and Collin Bates, Judy and Paul Wharton." She paused so that Sam could get the names down. "And Maude Ross and Walter Gibbons."

At the mention of the last couple, Morgan gave up trying to control her face and hooted involuntarily. Corky looked at her and said, "Oh, that's right, you know Maude!"

Morgan managed a nod.

"Has Dr. Richardson completed his session?" Sam asked Mrs. Hatfield when he and Morgan were back in the reception area after their revealing interview with Corky Vanderpelt-Richardson.

"Yes, he has." Mrs. Hatfield responded.

"Will you tell him we want to speak with him?"

"I'm sorry, I can't . . . "

"Just a minute here . . . ," Sam began.

Mrs. Hatfield interrupted, "I'm sorry, but Dr. Richardson just left."

"What?" Sam and Morgan said in unison.

"He said he had a pressing engagement," Mrs. Hatfield continued.

"Did he ask you to cancel the rest of today's clients?" Morgan asked.

Mrs. Hatfield stared at the papers on her desk for a moment. Still not looking up, she said, "Yes."

Morgan and Sam looked at each other. "If you hear from him," Sam instructed the older woman, "tell him to contact me at Central Precinct immediately."

☀ ☀ ☀

Sam and Morgan were regrouping at Coffee People. Sam was on his second chocolate brownie and second cafe latté. Morgan sipped her peppermint tea.

"Ugh! I feel a little sick." Morgan leaned back in her chair.

"So do I."

"You're sick from all the sugar you've downed in the last fifteen minutes." Morgan waved at the counter person to get her attention and held up two fingers, then pointed to her cup to order fresh tea for herself and a cup for Sam. "I'm sick from thinking about the Chandelier Club. Sometimes I can't believe what people do." The drinks arrived, and both sipped quietly for a few minutes.

"Something doesn't make sense to me," Morgan picked the conversation up again, and Sam set down his mug and looked at her. "If David killed Lucinda, why is Darrell Richardson acting so suspiciously?"

"I don't know." Sam started to add sugar to his tea. When he noticed Morgan's disapproving look, he put the shaker down. "I guess he figured Corky told us about the swinger's club, and he's embarrassed. Or maybe he's worried about client-therapist privilege if we want to ask him questions about David."

"Well, that's easily solved. Either David signs a release of information so you can talk to Richardson, or he refuses to. No, that wouldn't make him so skittish." Morgan took another swallow of tea. "I guess you're right, it's the club and probably the fact that he withheld that information from you in the first place." Morgan pushed her empty mug aside. "Well, I guess the case is essentially solved," she said glumly.

"Maybe not."

"What do you mean?"

"The shoes are still missing. David denies knowing anything about them. He says she kicked them off before pulling down her panty hose, but he doesn't remember anything about them afterwards."

"Do you think he's lying or has blanked it out?"

"I don't know. That's one of the things I wanted to ask Richardson about." Sam also pushed back his empty mug. "A search of David's room didn't turn them up or anything else unusual except lots of disposable enemas. I think that's another little quirk of David's. And a box of Sheiks."

"If David didn't take the shoes, who else could have or would have?"

"Ah, therein lies the mystery, Watson!"

"Wait a minute, Sherlock! Someone must have discovered Lucinda before I did! And for some weird reason took her shoes."

"Bingo!"

"So is that why you asked Corky for a membership list of their club? I thought maybe you were interested in joining," Morgan teased.

"Not my scene, but yes, I'm still working on the sexual angle with the shoes." Sam reached into his coat pocket. "Here, take a look at these names and tell me what you know about any of them."

Morgan opened up the folded piece of paper and read:

THE CHANDELIER CLUB

Norma and Collin Bates
Lucinda and Charles Frazier
Maude Ross and Walter Gibbons
Corky Vanderpelt-Richardson and Darrell Richardson
Judy and Paul Wharton

Morgan again had to stifle her glee.

"You recognize someone?"

"Do I ever! Maude Ross!"

"Who is she?"

"Maude is a former friend, emphasis on former. Walter Gibbons is her husband, although there are a large number of people who think he doesn't even exist, he's so forgettable. Come to think of it, Maude was at Lucinda's funeral."

"Was Walter there, too?"

"Beats me. I don't know what he looks like."

16

Later that evening, Morgan and Victoria were having a drink at Victoria's favorite hangout, Franny's, a mixed gay and lesbian bar. They were sitting at one of those microscopic tables that make people feel like Amazons and pushing fern tendrils out of the way so they could see each other. Moaning about managed care and the changes it was bringing to their practices had made them rather thirsty, so Victoria caught the waiter's eye and ordered a second margarita for herself and mineral water for Morgan.

"I want you to know you were wrong about Cynthia."

"Who?"

"The chemist. I didn't fall for her. I don't know anything about her toenails, but she had absolutely no sense of humor." Victoria leaned back in her chair. "How are April and Priscilla?"

"Priss is great. She's learning to swim. She's got the dog paddle down and can do a pretty good steamboat. The other day in the pool, she asked me to teach her everything I know about swimming, as though it would take fifteen minutes or so."

Morgan chomped a few ice chips. "April's very busy with a trial. She's representing Northwest AIDS Project. They're suing a billboard company for not accepting their ads about AIDS prevention."

"Why won't they display the ads?"

"Probably homophobia. NAP designed this really cute poster of a hunky guy wearing a yellow rain slicker and matching boots. Nothing else. The caption reads, 'Good boys always wear their rubbers.' I guess the billboard company thought it was too racy." Morgan sipped her fresh drink. "So NAP tried some more discreet ones, and they still wouldn't run them. April thinks NAP has a good chance of winning."

"I hope so," said Victoria. "I guess congratulations are in order, eh? You and that detective solved Lucinda's murder. *The Oregonian* is full of all the details of the guy's confession and his sexual problems."

"Ugh! I haven't read the paper yet, but I heard about the story. I'm surprised David's lawyer let him give an interview." Morgan popped a handful of peanuts into her mouth. "You know, I still don't think he's guilty."

"But he confessed!"

"I know. I guess I'm being silly. But I just can't imagine David writing that threatening letter to me."

"Did he admit doing it?"

"He says he doesn't remember doing it, but he could have."

"Did the police find any cut-up magazines at his house?"

"No."

"Well, who else would have?"

"You've got me. Maybe whoever took Lucinda's shoes also sent the letter and is the real murderer."

"What a strange souvenir!" Victoria finished her drink. "How much time elapsed between Lucinda's final good-bye and your hello?"

"The coroner says death occurred sometime between eight and ten in the morning, and I arrived right at noon. David said he left about nine. Someone else could have gone into her office any time during that three hours."

"What about her nine-thirty and ten-thirty clients?"

"Sam says the nine-thirty cancelled the day before. And the ten-thirty never showed."

Victoria slurped the last of her drink and then asked, "How come? Sounds suspicious to me."

"According to Sam, the woman couldn't find a parking spot, got frustrated, drove to Washington Park, and took a walk instead."

"No alibi, eh?"

"Apparently not. Sam doesn't think she was involved, though."

"How come? Does she have an adorable smile and a big bosom?"

"An adorable smile, probably. I don't know about the bosom. She's seventy-six. Besides, Sam says women never strangle people."

"Sounds a bit sexist to me."

Morgan sat back in her chair and ran her fingers through her hair. "I have a member of the Chandelier Club in mind for murderer."

"Huh? What's the Chandelier Club?"

"Settle back, Vic, this is really juicy."

17

Victoria listened raptly to Morgan's account of the Chandelier Club and its members. As they were splitting the check, Victoria exclaimed, "Don't look now, but two of your favorite people have walked in . . . together."

"Maude Ross and Newt Gingrich?"

"No. I wasn't being sarcastic. It's Donald and your detective friend. No! Don't look!"

"What? Why don't you want me to look?"

"Let's just watch for a few minutes before we say hello."

"This is silly." But Morgan turned slowly in her chair and saw Sam and Donald take a table in a corner. She noticed that each was very carefully dressed. Donald was really a very handsome man. Tonight he was wearing a silk turtleneck under a double-breasted navy sports coat. Sam, too, looked very spiffy. In fact, Morgan thought to herself, they make a very handsome . . . "Come on, Vic! Let's go!"

Morgan had thought to just slip out, but Victoria misunderstood her intent and was across the bar before Morgan caught up. "Hi, boys!" Victoria greeted them.

Sam was startled and started choking. "Hi, Victoria. Hi,

Morgan." Donald said. He was grinning from ear to ear. "Didn't expect to run into you."

"I guess not!" Morgan said a little more loudly and emphatically than she had intended. "How long has this been going on?" She unsuccessfully tried to sound casual.

"Hello, Morgan," Sam finally managed. "It's nice to see you, too. Hello, Dr. Trimbell."

"This may not make any sense to you, but I'm feeling a little betrayed. Why didn't you two let me know you were seeing each other?" Morgan looked from Sam to Donald.

"Sam and I have been dating since you first brought him home for dinner." Donald's red face looked both pleased and embarrassed. "I don't know why we didn't say anything to either you or April. I guess we just wanted our privacy for awhile."

"Of course you did. And I'm sure you do now, too," said Victoria. "Morgan and I were just on our way out."

"I'm just shocked, that's all." Morgan ran her hands through her hair. "But naturally I don't disapprove and . . . " At that moment Sam's beeper went off. He excused himself and went looking for a phone.

"Keep me company for a minute," Donald said, pulling up an extra chair. "I hear you're moving your office, Victoria," Donald remarked as the two women seated themselves.

"Yes. Corky is working hard to make me feel welcome. I think we're becoming friends. Darrell's okay when you get to know him, and Mrs. Hatfield is a gem."

"Corky's office is certainly, uh, unique," Morgan commented.

"Everything about Corky is unique. Have you seen her toenails?"

Donald and Morgan shook their heads.

"Well, she gets pedicures regularly, and she often has every nail done in a unique pattern. You know, stripes, polka dots, paisley."

"Paisley toenails! Wow!" said Donald.

Sam came hurrying up to the table. "I'm sorry, I've got to skip tonight, honey. Dr. Richardson has just shown up at Central Precinct. Do you want to come with me, Morgan?"

"Honey?" she muttered to herself. "Sure," she said to Sam.

✳ ✳ ✳

Darrell Richardson seemed considerably less composed sitting in an interrogation room at police headquarters than he had in his own office a few days before.

"Why'd you disappear yesterday afternoon?" Sam asked the man without preamble.

"I . . . I just needed to think things out."

"What things?"

"About Lucinda and David and everything." Richardson pinched the bridge of his nose between his thumb and forefinger.

"Everything?"

"My wife said she told you about the club."

"When did you talk to your wife?"

"A few hours ago. I called her from our beach house. I drove directly there when I left the office yesterday. After I talked to her, I came straight to you." Richardson was poking at the pressure points along his eyebrows. He must have a doozy of a headache, Morgan thought. "I know I should have told you about the club when you first questioned me."

"Why didn't you?" Morgan asked.

"I knew it couldn't have anything to do with Lucinda's murder, and if the club becomes public knowledge I could be ruined. So could my wife and perhaps some of the other members. And, besides, I was embarrassed." Richardson pulled a rumpled handkerchief from his breast pocket and began mopping his brow. "I'm fairly new to the world of swinging. Corky has introduced me to a lot of things. Before we married, I lived a rather sedate life." He gave a weak smile, which showed his big, even teeth.

"Look, Detective Reynolds. I'm very sorry for my behavior. I know I shouldn't have run out on you yesterday. I just had to think it through. But now I'm ready to answer any questions you might have."

"Let's start with David. Here's an information release form he signed allowing you to spill your guts to me." Sam handed Richardson a piece of paper. The psychiatrist fished a pair of designer glasses out of his shirt pocket and read the document carefully. "Tell me everything he told you about the day Dr. Frazier was killed. Don't leave anything out."

Darrell Richardson gave a long account of David's story which revealed nothing new.

"Do you believe he did it?" Sam asked.

"Yes. David is a very troubled young man. I think he killed Lucinda Frazier."

"Why?"

Dr. Richardson gave a long explanation of the oedipal process. "Basically, he couldn't handle the conflict between viewing Dr. Frazier as both a mother figure and a lover," he concluded.

"When David talked to me, he wasn't sure whether he had killed her or not. Now he's sure, and he says you helped him sort it out. What exactly did you do?" Morgan asked her colleague.

"The same thing you would have done if you had continued on the case, Dr. McRain. I simply helped him to distinguish between fantasy and reality." Morgan thought his voice sounded a little patronizing. "He wished he would have dreamed the murder. In reality, he's guilty."

"You have no doubt?" Sam asked.

"None."

"Do you work with fetishes?" Sam changed the subject. Morgan thought she saw a fresh line of sweat spring from Darrell's hairline.

"Yes, but . . . "

"Are you familiar with foot fetishes?"

"Yes, but what does this have to do with David?"

"I'll ask the questions." Sam loosened the knot on his tie. "First, are a foot fetish and a shoe fetish the same thing?"

"No. Often a person will have both fetishes but not always."

"If a person has a shoe fetish, what exactly do they do with shoes?" Sam inquired.

"It varies. For some people, and these are usually men, although not exclusively, just the sight of a shoe is a turn-on. Some use shoes in sexual acts. Ejaculating into the shoe, urinating into the shoe, rubbing the shoe over certain body parts, this sort of thing." Dr. Richardson seemed more relaxed and more matter-of-fact; he was an authority now, instead of a fugitive.

"Would a person with a shoe fetish collect shoes?" Sam wanted to know.

"Oh, certainly. I would think such a person would likely have a substantial collection."

"Does anyone in the Chandelier Club have a shoe collection?"

"Not to my knowledge."

"Where were you between eight and ten the morning Lucinda Frazier was murdered?"

"I was in my office all morning doing paperwork. Mrs. Hatfield can vouch for that. You know how it is, Dr. McRain, what with all these insurance billings, treatment plans, and that sort of thing." Morgan nodded. She knew how it was.

18

When Morgan wandered into the kitchen the next morning, rubbing the sleep from her eyes, she saw a happy domestic scene. April, Priss, Donald, and Sam were all enjoying Belgian waffles with sour cream and strawberries. Seeing Sam, Morgan pulled her robe closed a little tighter.

"Good morning, sleepyhead," everyone chorused. This was probably Donald's idea.

"Good morning, family," she returned. She gave Priss a peck on her sticky cheek and did the same to April. In a spirit of goodwill, she continued on around the table, kissing Donald and Sam. She poured coffee into a thick yellow mug and sat down.

"There are waffles in the oven for you," Sam said.

"Thanks. I need a minute to wake up first."

"Seymore! Mommy and Uncle Donald and me are going to the planetarium today to look at stars. Do you want to come?" Priss asked through a mouthful of strawberries and waffle.

"Thanks, sweetie. That really sounds like fun. But Sam and I have some people to talk to, and it looks like we'll get an early start." She raised her eyebrows at Sam.

"Might as well, but I'd like to stop by my place and grab a clean shirt."

"Fine. I'd love to see your place. Donald hasn't told me a thing about it," Morgan teased. "Who shall we start with?"

"Let's start at the beginning of the list with Norma and Collin Bates."

"I don't get it. The case seems pretty well wrapped up. Why are you still at it?" April wanted to know.

"Something just doesn't feel right about it," answered Sam as he stirred a third teaspoon of sugar into his coffee. "I just have to satisfy my curiosity."

Within an hour, Sam pulled up in front of a large gray stucco house. A few minutes later, the front door was answered by a trim woman with dark red hair and a cautious smile.

"Detective Reynolds and Dr. McRain," Sam said. "Are you Norma Bates?"

"Yes. What's this about?"

"Is your husband home, ma'am?"

"He was just leaving to play golf. It's his day off. Come in, and I'll catch him." She went down a hallway calling, "Collin! Collin!" A minute later Norma Bates returned with a tall, fleshy man wearing Bermuda shorts and argyle kneesocks.

"Detective," Bates thrust out his hand toward Sam. "I'm Collin Bates." He and Sam shook hands. Taking the initiative, Morgan grabbed his hand and pumped vigorously as she introduced herself.

"How can we help you?" Bates asked.

"May we sit down?" Sam asked.

"Of course." Collin remembered his manners and showed them to the living room, which was done in shades of mauve and turquoise.

When everyone was seated, Sam said, "We want to ask you a few questions about Lucinda Frazier and the Chandelier Club." Norma became interested in some lint on her skirt, and Collin paled.

Still picking at some invisible lint, Norma collected herself enough to say, "We hardly knew Lucinda outside of the club gatherings. She and Charles were not particular friends of ours."

"So you never saw her outside of club functions?" Sam questioned. Norma shook her head.

"Actually, I did . . . once. Professionally, that is," Collin said. "You see, I'm a dermatologist, and she came to me once about having a mole removed."

"Where?" Morgan asked.

"In my office, of course." Morgan frowned. "Oh, oh, I see what you mean. Well, it was on the top of her foot, actually. Right one, I think. Strange place for a mole really."

"Was there anything unusual about her feet?" Morgan persisted.

"No, not really." Collin frowned in memory. "Well, she did mention something about having to have her shoes custom made. Apparently her heel was very narrow, and the toes particularly wide. In fact, it was her cobbler who had recommended having the mole removed. He said it interfered with his designs."

"I don't suppose she mentioned the name of the cobbler?" Sam asked.

"No, sorry."

"Did both of you sleep with Lucinda?" Sam changed the subject.

"Certainly not!" Norma seemed truly shocked. "I don't know what you've heard about the club, but its activities are certainly not kinky! We don't go in for homosexuality or, or . . . "

"Bestiality or necrophilia or anything like that. Just good old-fashioned mate-swapping." Morgan finished Norma's sentence.

"Yes, that's right. I'm glad you understand." Norma smiled warmly at Morgan.

"Suppose you tell us exactly what does go on at your, er meetings." Sam said.

"We take turns meeting at one another's houses. Usually once a month on a Saturday night," Norma began. "We start with cocktails."

"And we discuss any new business or rule changes at that time," Collin added. "Actually, we have very few rules. No kids in the house. Stay with the same partner all evening. Don't have the same partner two times in a row. Don't leave the house. Use protection. And don't partner with your own spouse."

"Don't partner with your own spouse?" Morgan repeated.

"What would be the point?" Norma asked.

12

As they were pulling away from the Bates's house, Sam's phone rang. He answered it, listened a moment, and said, "Be right there." He replaced the receiver, saying to Morgan, "We've had a piece of luck. We've located the cobbler who made Lucinda's shoes. Let's go talk to him."

A few minutes later, they pulled up in front of a small shop in Old Town. It had a red awning across the front and on the window was painted "Ye Olde Cobbler Shoppe."

"Cute shoppee," Morgan said.

"Very," Sam agreed as he pulled open the red-painted door with a basket of red and white geraniums attached to it. Inside, the store had an exhibit of antique lasts on one wall and a display of various boots, pumps, dress shoes, and sandals, which were all beautifully crafted, on another. In front of the back wall was a high counter. The shop seemed deserted, but they soon heard, "Hold your horses! I'll be right there!" A small, white-haired man emerged from an open doorway behind the counter. He could barely see over the counter until he boosted himself onto a high stool.

He pulled a pair of rimless glasses from his forehead onto the bridge of his nose. He ignored Sam and, peering at Morgan, said, "What can I do for you, missy?" in a very gravelly voice.

Sam pulled open his badge, thrust it in the old man's face, and said, "We're here on official police business."

"Don't get your dander up, sonny." He pushed the badge back at Sam. "I suppose you want to talk about that dead woman. I got a call from one of your buddies. Let me get my records." He clambered off the stool and disappeared into the back room. Five minutes later, he reappeared carrying a big black, leather-bound book, which looked to be as old as the man himself, and a pair of emerald green pumps.

"These are beautiful!" Morgan exclaimed as the cobbler handed them to her and perched himself on the stool again. "Did you make these for Dr. Frazier?" she asked, running her fingers around one exquisitely made shoe.

"Sure did!" said the man as he placed the book on the counter and turned several pages until he found what he was looking for. "Damn shame, too."

"What do you mean?" Morgan asked.

"Waste of time and money. Nobody's going to wear them now."

"Oh, you mean they won't fit anyone else."

"That's right. See this large toe box and narrow heel," he said, taking the shoe from Morgan and using his finger to illustrate. "Never find another woman who could wear this shoe."

"They're awfully big for most women, too," Morgan sympathized.

"Nonsense!" the old man said sharply. "They're about an eleven. Most women wear their shoes a couple of sizes too small." He peered over the counter at Morgan's feet. She was glad she had on her sensible Rockport dress flats. "What size are these?" He scrambled off the stool and came from behind the counter. "Eight-and-a-half." He didn't wait for Morgan to answer. He plunked his surprisingly large thumb over her right big toe and pushed down. "You need a ten."

"Can we get back to Dr. Frazier?" Sam asked.

"Keep your pants on." The old man returned to his perch

and ran a finger down several columns in his book. "What do you need to know?"

"How many pairs of shoes did you make for her?"

"Let's see here." His eyes followed his finger back up the columns. "She started coming in about two years ago, and including these green pumps, twenty-six pair." Morgan whistled. "'Course, they weren't all shoes. That includes several pairs of boots, some sandals, and even some bedroom slippers."

"I'll need a copy of her orders," Sam said.

"Okay, sonny," he removed the page from his ledger. "Take this to the copy shop in the next block up. I'll keep your pretty friend here for security." He winked at Morgan.

When they were back in the car, Sam grinned, "I suppose you ordered a pair while I was gone?"

"I would have loved to, but I can't afford them. They start at two-fifty a pair, and the ones I really liked were almost four hundred." Sam interjected a whistle. "Lucinda spent somewhere around eight thousand dollars on shoes in two years!" Morgan concluded. "I think I need to talk to April about increasing my wardrobe allowance."

"I think we should get on with our interviews," Sam said. "Let's skip to Maude Ross and Walter Gibbons. I suspect we'd like to avoid them."

"The 'we' is generous, Sam." Morgan fastened her seat belt. "You're right, though. I have mixed feelings about seeing her. It'll be kind of fun telling her we know about the Chandelier Club, but I warn you, the woman's a shark, and it's hard not to get bitten around her."

"Never fear, I'll protect you," Sam pulled out into traffic.

"Watch your own crotch," Morgan responded.

※ ※ ※

Morgan didn't know whether it would be best to try her at the office or at home. Like many therapists, Morgan took Wednesdays off, but she wasn't familiar with Maude's schedule. They decided to try her house first. Sam rang the doorbell of the large saltbox in the Irvington neighborhood. The bell's ring echoed for a few minutes before a Walter Mitty look-alike answered it.

"Walter Gibbons?" Sam asked.

The man took off his glasses and wiped them on the sleeve of his gray sweatshirt. "Sorry. Steamed. Yes, I'm Walter Gibbons. How may I help you?"

Sam made the introductions. "We're investigating the murder of Dr. Lucinda Frazier, and we'd like to ask you a few questions."

"Please come in." Walter held the door open for them, but before they could enter, a whirlwind about Priss's size whipped through the doorway, kicked Sam in the shin, and ran off the porch into the yard.

Sam hopped up and down on one foot. Walter went in fast pursuit of the child. "Little monster ought to be locked up," Sam said quietly to Morgan before Walter returned with his son in tow.

"I'd like you to talk to this man about why you behaved with so much hostility toward him," Walter said to the boy, who was squirming to get away.

"No!" the boy screamed and slammed a foot on top of his father's instep. Walter repeated Sam's dance, releasing the child who ran into the house and slammed the door.

"Jeffrey! Open this door immediately!" No response. "How about if we just sit on the steps and talk. Jeffrey seems to need some space."

"That isn't all that kid needs!" Sam couldn't help himself.

"I'm sorry, Detective. I know Jeffrey is a little high-spirited. He takes after his mother. But we do believe in letting him express himself."

"Look, Mr. Gibbons, I deal every day with adults who have 'expressed' themselves in inappropriate ways. I think you should do some thinking about that. But, we really didn't come to discuss child rearing. Tell us about your relationship with Lucinda Frazier. And just so we don't waste any time, we know all about the Chandelier Club, and we've already interviewed other members."

Walter took off his glasses again, and this time he pulled a handkerchief out of the pocket of his corduroy pants, breathed on each lens and gave them a good polish. He replaced his glasses and looked at Sam. "I really don't know what to tell you. I liked Lucinda. I was shocked when I heard about her death."

"Why weren't you at the funeral?" Morgan wanted to know.

"I wanted to go, but Maude said it was important to her, and we try not to leave Jeffrey in day care any more than is absolutely necessary. We talked about taking him, but we decided next year is probably soon enough to begin exploring the death experience."

Morgan almost choked. She caught herself and continued with, "What do you do?"

"Do? Oh, for a living, you mean. Actually, I don't have to do anything. Family money. I keep busy studying ancient languages and, more recently, child development theories."

"Can you think of anyone who would want to kill Lucinda?" Sam asked. He was still rubbing his shin.

"Of course not, Detective. I don't know any murderers. Or at least, I hope I don't. Didn't I read that you'd arrested one of her clients for the crime?"

"That's right, but we just have to make sure. Now, please tell us all about your involvement with the club."

"Well, you see, I tend to be a bit reclusive, so Maude and I don't socialize very much. In many ways, we live very separate lives, but it suits us. Maude worried, though, because we didn't seem to have any common interests, besides Jeffrey, of course. So we tried various things: fly fishing, yodeling classes, kite flying, bungee jumping. None of them worked for both of us. Then she heard about the club. It was just forming. As a matter of fact, I think it was Lucinda who told her about it.

"Well, we tried it, and we both liked it. Theoretically, we both believe in open marriage, but Maude is better at meeting people than I am. She's a definite extrovert. She loves people, and people are drawn to her. I'm more introverted myself. But at the club there's an even number, so I never get left out." Walter paused to clear his throat a couple of times. "I know it may seem a little shocking to hear about, but it really doesn't hurt anyone. I think it's done me a world of good."

"So, you'd recommend swinging?" Morgan asked.

"Well, yes, I guess I would. I think everyone in the club has benefited."

"Except Lucinda," Sam added dryly.

21

Walter Gibbons told Sam and Morgan that his wife would be home in about an hour, so they decided to take a lunch break.

"I think it's time for you and me to have a little heart-to-heart, Morgan," Sam said between tortilla chips while waiting for their enchiladas to arrive.

"About your relationship with Donald?"

"No."

"About my relationship with April?"

"No."

"About our friendship?"

"No." Morgan started to open her mouth again, when Sam said, "Stop guessing. I'll tell you. I think you should fill me in on your relationship with Maude Ross."

"Oh." Morgan swirled a chip around in the salsa. She abandoned it and picked up another one and did the same thing. Five chips later, Sam said, "You don't want to talk about it?"

"Oh." Morgan seemed to see the chips for the first time. She fished them out of the salsa, deposited them in an ashtray, and kept staring at them. "We don't really have a relationship.

Well, not anymore at least. It's just that it's all so long ago, and I've made my peace with her. Well, not with her exactly, but with myself." Morgan looked at Sam. "She just keeps cropping up in my life."

Morgan was rescued for a few minutes as their food was placed before them. "I'm not really avoiding you, Sam, and I guess telling you this story would give you some perspective on Maude. It's just hard to organize it into a coherent whole." Morgan wrapped strings of cheese around her fork. "In a nutshell, Maude and I were in grad school together. We shared a field placement. We became lovers, but I was really looking for a mother at the time. I hadn't even sorted out my sexuality yet. I don't know what Maude was looking for."

Morgan took a few bites before continuing. "It was a dreadful relationship. I felt extremely controlled. I finally broke it off, and we've been leery of each other ever since."

Sam looked up when Morgan stopped talking. "Is that all?" he asked.

"Except that I think she's a terrific bitch, and I tend to like people who agree with me and mistrust those who don't." Morgan grinned wryly. "She's sort of a litmus test. Isn't that enough?"

"It's just that you've turned what was probably a really juicy story into a summary suitable for the evening news. Don't you know me well enough to dish a little dirt?"

"I'm sorry, Sam. It's not that I don't trust you, but you haven't exactly let me in on your own personal secrets—for example, Donald."

"Touché." Sam was quiet for a few minutes. "Okay. Fair is fair. Let me ask you a few questions about Maude, and then I'll tell you anything you want to know about me and Donald." Morgan nodded. "Was Maude your first female lover?"

"Yes, my first lover period. I guess I was a late bloomer. Before we became sexual, Maude used to worry out loud that people would think we were lesbians because we were so close, but that went right over my head."

"I can certainly relate to being so shut down around the whole thing that you never even apply the concept of homosexuality to yourself."

"Exactly. Even after Maude and I became lovers, I didn't think I was a lesbian. I just thought I was in love with Maude."

"Were you?"

"Yes. But it wasn't a very mature love. I was desperate to love somebody and have someone love me. Loving Maude, however, presented more problems than it solved."

"What do you mean?"

"Well, first of all, she didn't want us to tell anyone. She's terrifically homophobic, even though she wants everyone to see her as this great liberal. That was really a strain for me. Another problem was that even though I kept loving her, I gradually discovered I didn't like her."

"That would be a problem."

"Yes. I was in a lot of pain and conflict around it for a long time. I guess the thing that finally let me know I had to get out was what I mentioned before: Maude is a very self-centered, controlling woman. I didn't see that for a long time, but when I did, I couldn't see anything else.

"I felt like I was dying as a person. Actually, more like being consumed by Maude. She used to rip out pages from magazines like *Vogue* and give me the assignment of duplicating that particular look: hair, makeup, clothes." Morgan pushed away her plate. "Ugh! I felt like a possession."

"I think I get the picture." Sam reached across the table and took Morgan's hand. "It's okay, we don't have to talk about her anymore."

"Yeah, and I don't have to even think about her for all of about twenty minutes. After Maude, coming out wasn't that hard. It was fun exploring the lesbian bars, figuring out the sex and the politics."

"Did April come next?"

"No. I had to make up for lost time before I was ready to settle down. I think I had to relive adolescence since I was busy trying to avoid it the first time around." Morgan stared intensely into Sam's green eyes. "Now it's your turn. Are you serious about Donald?"

"Hopelessly."

"Is he your first male lover?"

"Well, there were those circle jerks when I was thirteen. Let's just say I've been around the block a few times."

"So, what does that mean?"

"I think it's time I made a confession. I've had my eye on Donald for awhile, but I was too chicken to introduce myself. At Gay Pride Day last year, I saw Donald, April, Priss, and you together. So, when I met you again at Lucinda's office, I thought maybe . . . "

"You could kill two birds with one stone. Get information from me, and use me to meet Donald."

Sam looked at his plate. "It sounds pretty rotten when you put it like that, but it's true. I'm sorry. I've been feeling guilty about it, especially since we've become friends."

"I thought maybe you were, uh, interested in me. Especially after you introduced me to your mom. That's when I knew I had to tell you about April."

"I'm not out to my family. And frankly, I did enjoy flirting with you. I felt a spark, too. I don't think these things are usually one-sided, and if we were both het, who knows?"

"Well." Morgan ran her hand through her hair. "I'm glad you told me. I think having another brother is nice. You certainly make Donald happy. By the way, when did you and Donald first do it?"

A flush creeped up from Sam's collar to his forehead. "I'm pleading the fifth on that one."

"Come on! Fair is fair! You said I could ask you anything."

"I lied."

22

Morgan involuntarily let out a big sigh as Sam stopped in front of the same house for the second time that day. Maude Ross was standing on the porch. She stood very straight with her arms folded across her chest. Looking up at her from street level, Morgan thought she appeared to be a giant. It wasn't her size but her personality that made her look so huge. She was only five feet tall, but she always wore heels that added another three or four inches.

Maude invariably dressed to be noticed, as though there was some danger she wouldn't be. Today she wore a purple silk suit, yellow blouse, and boots. Her jet black hair was a sleek cap on her head.

Morgan realized her own outfit was totally beige. She sighed again as she clambered out of the car and followed Sam up the porch steps.

"I've been waiting for you," Maude said in a voice that would make anyone from a small child to senior citizen feel guilty.

Sam ignored the statement and started to pull out his badge.

"Never mind. I know who you are. And I know what you want. What I want to know is, how did you get into playing at detective, Morgan? First it was your little adventure into teaching, and now this. One would think private practice wasn't fulfilling enough for you."

"What's fulfilling to me at this moment is getting to question you. Tomorrow I think I'll try bungee jumping. Remind me before we leave to ask you for some tips."

"May we come in?" Sam asked.

"No. My son is napping."

"Perhaps you'd be more comfortable talking to us at Central Precinct," Sam countered.

"I'll just get some deck chairs." Maude went into the house.

"Morgan, let me ask the questions," Sam whispered.

Before Morgan could reply, Maude returned with Walter, who was carrying three yellow director's chairs. He set them down, unfolded them, and retreated into the house. "Now, Detective. I am available."

"How well did you know Lucinda Frazier?"

"We were good friends. We met at a professional meeting just after she moved here a couple of years ago. We had common interests, so we'd do lunch once or twice a month."

"What kind of common interests?"

"Psychotherapy, of course, and child rearing."

"Tell us about her relationship with her husband."

"I don't know much, really. I know it was Lucinda's idea to separate, but she didn't give me any specifics. I just assumed that they had grown apart."

"You know Charlie was married before?"

"Lucinda told me that Charlie was a young widower when they first met. His wife died in an unusual accident. Apparently she was into birding and fell off some cliff on the coast. They had lived here before Charlie moved to Boston. Lucinda hadn't been married before."

"Your husband told us that it was Lucinda who invited you to join the Chandelier Club."

"That's right."

"Tell us more."

"About the club? Well, Walter and I were searching for activities that we could share and weren't having much luck. I told Lucinda about our plight, and she told me about the club. It was just forming. Apparently it was Corky Vanderpelt's idea. She convinced Darrell, and Darrell told Lucinda." Morgan noticed that, other than Maude's mouth, not a muscle in her face was moving. Morgan knew this was one of Maude's ways of handling anxiety, by staying in control. If you can't control anything else, control your facial muscles.

"Was there anything unusual that went on in the club?" Sam asked. This question surprised Morgan because she thought everything about the club was unusual.

"I'm sure I don't know what you mean, Detective."

"Anyone have any problems with jealousy? Anyone harbor any resentments? You're a psychologist. You would have noticed these things."

"Of course. I suppose this could be important, but I'm not sure how. I think Judy Wharton felt threatened by Lucinda. Judy has severe self-esteem problems, and I think she didn't like the fact that her husband, Paul, seemed quite drawn to Lucinda. It was all very subtle, and I'm not sure anyone else noticed, but I picked up on it. And at one point I think Judy tried to make a play for Charlie Frazier, but that seemed to fizzle."

"How did Judy and Paul Wharton get involved in the club?"

"I believe Charlie invited them. He and Paul have some business connection. Paul's an attorney." Maude had her legs crossed at the knee and was vigorously swinging her left foot.

"What sort of work does Judy Wharton do?" Sam asked.

"Oh, she's an artist. She mostly makes clay masks, rather gruesome looking, really. She has an exhibit at the library right now."

"Those are exquisite boots, Maude. Did you have them custom made?" Morgan asked.

"As a matter of fact, yes. Lucinda turned me on to a wonderful cobbler." At that moment, Jeffrey burst through the door wearing a cowboy hat, vest, chaps, and holsters. In each hand he held a carrot, which he pointed at them.

"Reach for the sky, partners!" he commanded.

Sam and Morgan thrust their hands into the air. "May I speak for you to these grown-ups, Jeffrey?" Maude asked her son. His silence seemed to indicate consent to Maude because she continued, "Naturally, we don't approve of violence in this household, but all little boys have a certain amount of aggression for which they must find suitable discharges. Therefore, we allow him to use carrots instead of toy guns. Of course, we want him to recognize the absurdity in all of this, so an appropriate response for you to make would be, 'I see your carrots, cowpoke, but I'm not afraid.' You're free to paraphrase, of course."

Jeffrey seemed used to this kind of nonsense. He stood with his carrots drawn throughout his mother's lengthy explanation. Morgan felt confused. She wanted to respond to the child but refused to participate in Maude's weirdness. Sam looked completely dumbfounded. No one did anything for a moment, then Morgan, with her hands still in the air, stretched her face toward the boy and took a big bite off of one of the carrots. Jeffrey laughed and stuck the other carrot in his mouth.

23

Morgan, April, Donald, and Priss were taking a family day at Cannon Beach on Thursday. They had cleared their schedules weeks ahead in order to avoid the weekend crowds. And since it was a blustery day in March, the beach was practically deserted. Sam had been invited along, but he had some pressing business on another case.

They were taking advantage of a break between rainstorms to try their luck at flying kites.

"I'm glad you thought of this, Morgan. We haven't flown kites in years," April exclaimed as she put her double trick kite through its paces.

Morgan watched her huge pink-and-purple delta soar higher and higher. "You can thank Maude Ross. She gave me the idea. Or rather, her husband did." Morgan turned to see Priss running along with a tiny red pocket kite in the air behind her. Donald was even further away, holding the string of a silvery dragon kite with a long tail that whipped in and out as it sailed.

"What'd Sam think of Maude?" April called as she let out a little more string.

"He simply couldn't believe her! I tried to prepare him ahead of time, but it really is hard to explain Maude. You just have to experience her."

"Sort of like horehound candy."

"Huh?"

"When I was little my father tried to tell me how it tasted, but I insisted on trying it. Believe me, once was enough. I feel the same way about Maude Ross," said April. Morgan knew that April's dislike of Maude was mostly out of loyalty to Morgan. In return, Morgan disliked April's ex-lovers—the professional tennis player and the politician who sold out on feminism to get elected to the state senate.

Priss came running up. She was furiously reeling in her little kite. "Seymore! I'm ready to fly a big kite now! Can I fly yours?"

"Sure, honey. Let's get your kite in first." Morgan reeled in the red kite. "Okay, I'm going to stick it in the big zip pocket of your parka so we won't lose it. Now you can take hold of mine. There you go. Let the string out easy." Morgan watched Priss's face glow with excitement as the big pink-and-purple kite soared through silver skies. Sighing happily, she looked over to see April watching her and smiling. They failed to notice that the delta was into making friends with the twin trick kite.

"Uh-oh!" Priss said.

April and Morgan looked up. Their kites were involved in an intimate dance, weaving around and around each other. "Looks like a mating ritual," April observed.

"Looks like trouble to me," Morgan said dryly. Sure enough, a moment later, the kites plunged into the wet sand.

"I'm going to go help Uncle Donald," Priss called as she ran away from the mess.

"Good idea," Morgan mumbled as she tried to figure out where to begin the disentanglement.

The two women worked together in silence for several minutes, untying knots and winding up string, before April said, "Morgan! I forgot to tell you. While you were out getting the bagels this morning, Sam called. He said to tell you that they compared the cobbler's records with Lucinda Frazier's closet and were able to determine that there were only two pairs of shoes missing."

"Two pairs?"

"Yes. Gray suede and black calf."

"I wonder where the other pair is?"

"Ah, that particular mystery is solved. Sam thought to check with the mortician, and sure enough, she was buried in black calf pumps."

The kites were finally separated and declared fit to fly again. Both women were busy rigging up the stringing when the skies opened up and drenched them. They started running toward Priss, who joined them. Donald waved them on, as he was trying to gather up his soggy dragon. Soon all four were safe and dripping in the van.

"This calls for hot tea and oyster stew!" Donald announced.

"Are oysters the ones I like?" Priss asked.

"I don't know, sweetie. We'll just have to see," answered April. After a short drive to Dooger's Cafe the family was seated in a wooden booth, slurping up buttery oyster stew and waiting for clam fritters.

"Donald," Morgan began, "I have the keys to the van in my pocket, and it's still pouring out, so I suggest you tell us all about your relationship with Sam. Don't leave out any of the good parts."

"This detective stuff is turning you into a pushy person, Morgan. I feel like one of your interrogees."

"Sorry, Donald, but I want the facts and nothing but the facts." Morgan did her best to imitate the Dragnet character.

"Okay, okay. I should thank you for bringing him home. I felt like it was my lucky day."

The waitress arrived with plates of clam fritters and onion rings. As Morgan bit into a gigantic onion ring, she said, "Even if the weather doesn't clear, I've got to get in another walk on the beach to try and save my arteries before we head back."

"I don't think that's exactly how it works, but I'm with you just as soon as I sample the peanut butter pie," returned April.

Morgan groaned and added, "I hear the marionberry cobbler is fantastic." For several minutes the sound of rain pounding on the roof dominated. "Okay, Donald, let's hear it. There was Sam, and there was you, as I recall, lounging around in your kimono. Come to think of it, you changed into that after Sam arrived."

"Guilty. Those green eyes weren't wasted on me, and I could tell he was interested. Remember, he volunteered to help with dinner."

"I thought he was just trying to be nice," Morgan said.

"I thought he was just trying to adapt to the upside down rules of our house; you know, men do the cooking and cleaning up, women relax with drinks before dinner," April added. Donald stuck out his tongue at his sister.

"Anyway, when he followed me into the kitchen to get my recipe for cassoulet, I discovered that that wasn't all he wanted."

"What did he do?" Priss asked. All three adults looked at one another.

"He told me he liked my kimono. I told him he could try it on, and he did."

"You weren't wearing anything under that!" Morgan was shocked.

"I didn't say I was subtle," Donald returned. "Just effective." Priss nodded wisely.

24

On the way home, April drove, and Morgan sat in the passenger seat, gazing out the window. Donald and Priss were asleep in the back. After a long peaceful time listening to the windshield wipers, April said, "I want to ask you something, Morgan." Morgan turned to look at her partner. "Just exactly how many therapists do you think are sexually involved with their clients?"

"Seventy-three."

"What?"

"I'm teasing. But what kind of question is that? I can't tell you 'exactly' how many. Too many. How's that for an answer?"

"You know what I mean. Does it happen a lot? I'm thinking about Lucinda and David."

"I don't think it happens a lot, but if it happens at all, it's too much. And it does happen. Nearly always, however, it's male therapists with female clients." Morgan shook her head. "This thing with Lucinda is hard to believe, but I guess I've come to accept her having sex with David as a fact. The evidence is very compelling."

"Goddess! You're sounding more like a detective every

day." April squeezed Morgan's shoulder. "But it's okay. I think you have a knack for it. You think that Lucinda slept with David but that he didn't kill her. Am I right?"

"You're right, that's what I think."

"That's why you're pursuing the thing with the shoes with such energy?" Morgan nodded. "But why is Sam? Does he think the same thing?"

"I'm not sure. We haven't talked about it, but he's as interested in the shoes as I am."

"What about David's confession?"

"I don't know. At first, he wasn't even sure any of it happened. He thinks maybe he dreamed it. Then he's certain he slept with her and murdered her. I don't know," Morgan repeated herself. "I think he's very mixed up, and I'm not positive his sessions with Darrell Richardson really helped him all that much."

"They apparently helped him figure out that he really slept with her, and that part seems to be true, at least judging from the evidence of the condom."

"Yes, but just because he had sex with her doesn't mean he killed her."

"True. But who else?"

"Whoever took the shoes. No doubt the same person who sent me the threatening letter."

"But if that person is still at large, why aren't you getting any more warnings? You haven't stopped investigating."

"Perhaps whoever did it wants us to continue to believe David is guilty, so he wouldn't want to stir up any doubt by sending another letter."

"He?"

"Sam says women don't strangle. They use poison or guns. Not knives, either."

"What about Juliet?"

"Juliet?" echoed Morgan. "Of Romeo and Juliet?" April nodded. "Maybe suicide is different, but I doubt it. I think it's just that male authors like to attribute more violence to women than is real," said Morgan. "Like in mystery novels. As often as not, a woman did it. But in real life, of course, women almost never do it, statistically speaking."

"But what about Lucinda Frazier—who could have done it? Someone just happened to wander into her office when she was in a postcoital daze and strangled her? And where was David?"

"David told Sam that when he realized he had strangled her, he just ran out of the office, down the back stairs, and home to bed. That was part of why he thought he had dreamed it." April pulled around a slow-moving tractor. "That all rings true. I just don't think he killed her. I think when he realized he had made love to her successfully, it was very shocking for him, and that's when he ran out. He also said he thought he left the door to her office open as he ran out."

"So Lucinda's lying there in ecstasy, and someone comes in and strangles her? Why?" wondered April.

"Jealousy?"

"Seems like you better talk to Charles Frazier again."

"Except his alibi checked out. But we need to talk to him anyway. He didn't tell Sam about the Chandelier Club. Also, there's Paul and Judy Wharton."

"Who?"

"More members of the infamous club. Maude Ross thinks Paul had the hots for Lucinda."

"Are we there yet?" came a sleepy voice from the backseat.

"Not yet, Priss. Go back to sleep."

"I want a drink of water."

"We'll be there soon."

"I have to go to the bathroom."

"Can you wait, honey? We'll be there soon."

"I'm going to be sick."

The yellow van pulled to the side of the road.

25

Donald carried the sleeping Priss upstairs to bed. April was putting away kites and things. Morgan called her voice mail for messages to see if any of her clients were in crisis or needed to change their appointment times for tomorrow. The third message was from Sam.

April passed by as Morgan was scribbling furiously. "What's up?"

Morgan replaced the receiver and glanced at the clock. "It's Sam. He wants me to meet him at this address," she held up the scratch pad, "if I get home before eight. It's 7:45 p.m. now, so I guess I'll go."

"Where?"

"1741 SW Tyler Avenue. That must be in the section of town where all the streets are named for obscure presidents: Polk, Tyler, Van Buren."

"Right. And some day they'll add: Ford, Carter, Reagan, Bush, and maybe Clinton."

"I'm out of here." She gave April a quick hug.

Morgan didn't have any trouble spotting the address. Sam could have just said, drive up Tyler until you come to all the police cars. Morgan found a place to park and walked toward the big white, frame house, which was cordoned off with yellow crime-scene tape and a half dozen uniformed officers. She approached one and said, "Detective Reynolds asked me to meet him here."

"Stay put."

A few minutes later, Burly came bustling up. "Oh, it's you. Follow me." He led her up the front steps, through the house into a large, modernized, stark white kitchen. Morgan took in the white tile countertops, white tile floor, white walls, white cabinets. The only color in the room was a red-marked outline of a body in the center of the floor.

"Morgan! Thanks for coming." Sam came into the room from another door that seemed to lead to a back porch. Morgan remembered some of the same men who had dusted for prints and made photographs in Lucinda's office.

"Who . . . who . . . is, er, was that?" Morgan stuttered.

"Let's go into the dining room for a few minutes. I'm almost through here." Sam took Morgan by the shoulders and led her to a chair at the dining room table. "I called you because I think this is related to Lucinda's murder, and I knew you wouldn't want to be left out." Morgan nodded mutely. "The victim was Judy Wharton."

"But we were going to interview her tomorrow evening."

"I know. Maybe somebody didn't want us to. I don't really know why she died yet, but it's too much of a coincidence to think there's no relationship."

"That means David is innocent."

"I've thought so."

"Why didn't you say anything?" Morgan looked into Sam's eyes. "I was telling April just this afternoon that I think David slept with Lucinda but that he didn't kill her."

"That's how I've got it figured, too. That's why the shoes are so important."

"Are Judy's missing?"

"Yes. If she was wearing any. Since she was at home, it's harder to know. Also, she doesn't have hers custom made. The ones in her closet all have labels: Nike, Rockport, Birkenstock. You know, the usual yuppie brands."

"How did she die? And when?"

"Her sixteen-year-old daughter found the body about six o'clock."

"Poor kid!"

"Yeah, she's with her grandparents now. Judy was stabbed to death with a kitchen knife. It was pulled out of a knife block sitting right on the counter. So it probably wasn't premeditated."

"Were there signs of a struggle?"

"Yeah. Clumps of her hair were pulled out, and her t-shirt was torn. She had a heavy iron skillet in her hand, so she probably gave her killer a nasty wallop somewhere."

"Any prints on the knife? Was it found?"

Sam smiled. "The knife is still in the body. Either the killer got lucky, or he knew what he was doing. He plunged it right smack in the middle of the heart. And it was wiped clean of prints."

"Where's Paul Wharton?"

"That's the sixty-four-thousand-dollar question."

"You mean you don't know?"

"We checked with his office just after six. No answer. We got a hold of one of his partners in the office. She said he left about five, and there was nothing on his calendar for this evening. His daughter can't remember if he mentioned an appointment for tonight but said he often works late."

Burly came up to Sam at that moment and said, "He's here. I've got him in the living room. I told him what happened, and he's bawling like a baby." Sam and Morgan followed Perry into the front room. A big man wearing a tan raincoat over a dark three-piece suit sat on one of a pair of white sofas facing each other. He had his elbows on his knees, and his face was covered with big, well-groomed hands. A pair of glasses lay on the white carpet.

"Mr. Wharton? I'm Detective Reynolds. I'm in charge of this investigation, and I need to ask you a few questions." The man slowly sat up, removed his hands from his face, found a handkerchief in his jacket pocket, loudly blew his nose, wiped his eyes, and stared blankly from Sam to Morgan. Morgan handed him his glasses.

"Thanks." He wiped them too and replaced them on his face. "Who would kill Judy?"

"That's what we're trying to find out. When's the last time you saw your wife?"

"Actually, we met here for lunch at about one. We try to spend as much time together as possible because we both have busy schedules."

"When did you leave?"

"About two-fifteen."

"Was your wife here all afternoon?"

"As far as I know. She was working on a new series of masks. She was doing all of our friends. Her studio is the converted garage out back."

"How was she at lunchtime?"

"I'm not quite sure what you mean. She seemed normal. She was eager to get back to work when I left."

Sam got up to pace around the room a bit as though deep in thought before turning toward Wharton again, "Where did you go when you left your office this evening?"

"Surely that's not relevant to your investigation, Detective!" Wharton protested in an indignant voice.

"Just answer the question," said Burly.

"I did a little shopping at Pioneer Place Mall. I was looking for some sports shirts, but I didn't find anything to suit me. Then I stopped for a bite to eat at one of the concessionaires."

"Which one?"

"Cackleberry's. I had a chicken sandwich. Then I went to the library to find a new mystery. I wanted the new Kellerman, but it wasn't in. Neither was the new Hillerman. After that, I just came home."

"With no sports shirts and no novels?" Sam loosened his tie and sat back down again. "Tell me, Paul, is it usual for you to wander around on Thursday evenings?"

"Not really, but I knew Valerie had play rehearsal after school, and Judy wanted to work through the evening. We had agreed at lunch not to dine together tonight, so I was at loose ends."

"Okay. Tell me about Lucinda Frazier. We know about the Chandelier Club. And that you had an interest in Lucinda."

"Detective, my wife has just died! I don't want to talk about another woman. It's indecent!" There was a long pause. Finally, Wharton said, "All right! All right! Let's get this over with so I can go be with my daughter, for God's sake!" Wharton sounded angry, and there were fresh tears in his eyes. "Yes. I was drawn to Lucinda. That stupid club! When Charlie told me about it, I thought it seemed like a good idea. Except for the Richardsons, we'd all been married for a while, and well, you tend to fall into certain patterns. Our intimate relationship tended to have a lower priority than it should have." Wharton seemed to look for understanding. "I had to talk Judy into it. She was raised Catholic, although she hasn't attended services since we got married.

"At first, it did make our intimacy more exciting, until I started to fall for Lucinda. Then, I didn't really want to be with Judy sexually. I've come to think of her more as my partner and best friend, not my lover. We never discussed it, but I know she figured it out. It's been hell for me since Lucinda's death. I've been so depressed." The tears were flowing copiously. Paul didn't even try to hide them.

"Did Lucinda return your affection?" Morgan asked.

"She didn't take me seriously. She just told me I had some problems with my mother I needed to work out." Wharton cried harder.

"One last question," said Sam. "Did you run into anyone you know at the mall or at the library?"

"No. Should I have?"

"Yes."

 ✳ ✳ ✳

"So what happens next?" Morgan and Sam were winding down at the Original Hotcake House. They were sitting in a Day-Glo orange booth talking over a noisy jukebox being fed coins by a young man with hair the color of the booth.

Sam took another bite of apple pancake before answering. "Well, one thing for sure is we need to talk to Charlie Frazier again. We needed to before this; now we really do. Charlie didn't tell us about the club, and we also need to hear more about his relationship with Judy Wharton." Sam took another bite of the gooey stuff. Morgan used her own napkin to wipe a dribble off his chin.

"Thanks, Mom."

"Sorry. I guess I was thinking of Priss." Morgan sipped her peppermint tea and pushed her potatoes around with her fork. "Do you think Paul killed his wife?"

"I don't know, but his alibi is sure weak."

"If he killed Judy, he probably killed Lucinda, too, but he seemed to care so much for her."

"Ah! One of the best motives for murder there is . . . *amore*!"

"I suppose you're right. And he said Lucinda didn't take him seriously. If that's true, I'm sure it was wounding. But he seemed so genuinely upset about both of them."

"If you had murdered someone, wouldn't you be upset?"

"Of course, but . . . "

"I know what you're going to say, 'but I could never murder anyone.' I think you could."

"Gee, Sam, thanks a lot for the vote of confidence." Morgan was truly offended.

"I didn't just mean you, personally. As our esteemed Dr. Richardson said, I think anybody could under the right circumstances."

"You don't think you have to be completely sociopathic or at least a little bit crazy to kill?"

"No. Certainly sociopaths like Ted Bundy do kill, but the majority of murders are committed by ordinary people in

112

extraordinary circumstances." He waved an empty syrup bottle at the waitress. "Generally, incarcerated murderers are the best prisoners and, for the most part, present the least threat to society."

Morgan pushed away her almost-full plate. "Did you study criminology in college?"

"Guilty."

"So, what's the answer? Do we just say to someone who deprived another person of life, we understand you were under extraordinary stress. Please don't do it again."

"I think we start with not hitting children, so they don't grow up to act out their own frustrations."

"You sound like me." Morgan smiled at her friend. "Do you think Judy could have killed Lucinda in a jealous rage? Maybe she thought Lucinda had just been sleeping with Paul."

"Maybe. But then who killed Judy?"

"Paul. After he figured out that Judy strangled Lucinda."

"Maybe. Except, the fact that both the murdered women's shoes were missing would point to one murderer, not two. I think we'd better sleep on this. Are you free for lunch tomorrow?"

"Let's see." Morgan whipped out her Daytimer from the pocket of her parka. "Yes. I'm free from one to three. What do you have in mind?"

"Mom's pastrami sandwiches. I'll pick up a couple and meet you at the Whartons'. We'll take our time looking over things. We sealed the house, so nothing will have been disturbed."

"Could you make mine egg salad?"

26

Morgan awoke to strains of "Oh, What a Beautiful Morning!" April was singing in the shower. Separating herself from the covers, Morgan jerked to an upright position. Over thirty years of experience had taught her not to linger at this part of the process. It was just too easy to roll over and oversleep. She turned up one silver-pink miniblind to scope the weather scene. Rays of sun poked through the March clouds.

Thirty minutes later, Morgan was showered and pulling her fingers through still-damp curls as she made her way into the kitchen. It was strangely deserted. Morgan looked out the window and saw Donald and Priss in the sandbox. Buckets and shovels and plastic cars were in furious motion. Donald's long legs took up a great deal of the space.

April came up behind Morgan and wrapped her arms around her. "Priss is very lucky to have Donald," Morgan said. "Actually, we all are."

"Hmmmm. I just got off the phone with Mom. She wishes Donald would find a 'real' career."

"She'd like you to trade roles with him, wouldn't she? The

115

world would be as it should if Donald were the successful attorney and you were a mommy-homemaker. And to complete the picture, I should have a sex change!"

"That might please Mom, but definitely not me!" April pulled Morgan closer and kissed her passionately. "I've got to run. Kiss everyone good-bye for me."

⁂ ⁂ ⁂

Sam let himself and Morgan into the Wharton home. "I just keep hoping we weren't as thorough as we could have been last night."

It was a rambling old house that had been modernized in the last few years. Morgan hadn't really noticed much of the decor the night before, except for how white everything was. The living room had white carpet, white drapes, matching white sofas, and a brick fireplace, which had been painted white. There was a coffee table in white marble. The white was barely relieved by accents of bright blue: blue sofa pillows, a blue vase on the coffee table, and a grouping of blue ceramic figures on the mantel.

Morgan moved to the mantel and examined the figures. Each was an earth mother archetype with pendulous breasts, big abdomens, and a hole between her legs. One had an infant emerging from the hole, another was suckling an infant, two were embracing each other. "These are exquisite!" Morgan proclaimed. She turned one over carefully and found the initials "JW" carved into the base. "Maybe Judy had a different reason for being jealous," she said to Sam, who was poking around the fireplace.

Sam came over, examined the figures, and said, "Maybe. Let's move on to the dining room."

The dining room, too, was white on white. The accent color here was green. Sam looked through the china closet. Among the usual crystal and china were two ceramic platters and several bowls bearing the "JW" signature. Each had luminescent colors swirled on its surface. "She was really very gifted," Morgan remarked.

"Nothing significant here," Sam said, all businesslike. They went into the kitchen, where the blood-red outline on the floor made Morgan shiver. Judy had intended a different accent color. There were yellow kitchen towels, stacks of yellow fiestaware above the sink, and a cheerful yellow teakettle on the stove.

"I'm not very comfortable here," Morgan admitted. "Why don't I go check Judy's studio?"

"Fine," Sam said, without looking up.

Morgan went out the back door and followed a cement path to the detached building. Rhododendron and azalea bushes covered with a thin, melting layer of snow edged the path.

Morgan turned the knob, and the door opened onto a truly delightful room. A hand-braided cotton rug in bright blues, greens, and pinks covered a light oak hardwood floor. In one corner was an old potbellied stove and a couple of wooden rocking chairs. Another corner held a kiln and a potter's wheel. A long wooden table was nearby, beneath which stood large ceramic crocks containing different kinds of clays. Sculpting tools and various armatures sat on the table, all covered with a fine layer of clay dust.

Morgan's eyes were drawn up to the shelves that ran along two walls of the room. She froze. Above the shelves, which were overflowing with Judy's work, hung Lucinda Frazier. Or rather, a lifelike mask of Lucinda painted so realistically that Morgan's heart stopped. Beside Lucinda was Paul, next came Maude, Walter, Corky, Darrell, Norma, Collin, and finally Judy herself. Morgan recognized her from a photo on the mantel in the living room. "Someone's missing," Morgan said to herself.

She moved to the table, where something lay covered up with thick plastic. She carefully removed the plastic and screamed.

Within thirty seconds, Sam was panting at her side. She hadn't moved. "Morgan! What in the world . . ." Sam stopped, and they both stared at the unwrapped piece. It was the missing mask. Charlie Frazier was as lifelike as the rest of them, even though the mask hadn't been fired or glazed yet. But Charlie's face had been slit from brow to lip diagonally by a large knife.

27

"Who do you think slashed the mask?" Morgan asked after they had retreated to the dining room and silently unwrapped their sandwiches.

Sam licked the dripping side of his sandwich before answering. "Could have been Judy or anyone, I guess. Maybe even the murderer. I'll have the sculpting tools checked for prints."

"I don't think it was Judy. I can't imagine putting as much effort into creating something like that only to ruin it." Morgan crunched a dill pickle before continuing, "One thing is sure, whoever slashed the mask isn't too happy with Charlie Frazier." Sam nodded. "And what do you make of the placement of the masks on the wall? I don't think it's random."

"Paul told us she started with a mask of Lucinda, so it makes sense that her mask is first. Do you think she really molded it on Lucinda's face?"

"I don't know. It certainly looks lifelike. They all do."

"I guess we'll have to ask the 'groupies' about them."

Sam smiled. "I'll get a photographer out to take some shots of the masks. Meanwhile, let's draw a diagram of where they are on the wall." Sam pulled a notebook and pen from his inside jacket pocket. When he was done sketching, he opened a paper bag and shoved it toward Morgan. "Do you want some chips?"

"No thanks. The masks are paired up with the appropriate spouses, except Lucinda and Paul are together, and presumably, Judy and Charlie would have been, too." Morgan absent-mindedly picked up a chip. "Do you think Judy wanted to trade husbands with Lucinda?"

"If so, why would she have slashed poor old Charlie? If, in fact, she did?" Sam stuffed a handful of chips into his mouth.

"So far, this new development hasn't answered many questions, but it sure has left us with a lot of new ones." Morgan picked up another chip.

"There's something else I haven't told you about yet." Sam stuffed another handful of chips in his mouth. Morgan waited impatiently. "I found Judy Wharton's diary just before you screamed."

"Her diary?"

"Well, more like a journal, I guess. There aren't really dated entries. It's sort of like poetry. Love poetry. Love-sick poetry."

"Let me see," Morgan demanded. Sam handed her one of those blank-paged books with a flowered cover. She thumbed through several pages and said, "I see what you mean." She read aloud:

I want to hold you with open arms.
Not easy for me.
Sometimes my arms grasp with pure pleasure.
Sometimes they slip and drop with looseness.
Sometimes ache with holding.

I love you and I want you to love me.
That doesn't mean I want to own you.
That doesn't mean I want to be the only one you love.
Mostly what I want to tell you and me is don't
be scared or maybe don't run too far in your scare.

"Sounds like someone new to nonmonogamy to me. Oh, brother," said Morgan. She continued flipping through pages. "Uh-oh, the tide is turning. Listen to this:

> Stomach hurts with one-in-the-morning aloneness.
> I pulled into your drive and her car was there.
> I sped away. Where to go? What to do? I scream
> my anger and my throat hurts.
>
> I know all about her and why she's in your life.
> I needed you. When I need I want to run away
> because I feel so weak and I might be hurt.
> Now I don't want to see you ever.

"If only we knew who 'you' and 'she' were," said Morgan.

"I think we might be on to something. Let me see that again." Sam reached for the book, and Morgan relinquished it. He, too, flipped through several pages and read,

> You're with the other woman again tonight.
> I choose to be alone rather than be with
> someone when all my thoughts are with you.
>
> You tell me you love me and that you don't
> want to leave and yet you go.
> I struggle not to complain, cry, cling, yell.
> I succeed and feel empty.
> I am frozen here and can do nothing else.
> My love for you captures me.
> Come home lover.

"Come home? Do you think she's been writing about Paul?" Sam asked.

"I think she means 'home' more in a poetic sense. But I'm not sure. Poetry's not really my thing."

"You mean you don't write sonnets to April?"

"Only in the first six months. It was mandatory then."

28

Late Friday night, April and Morgan were cuddling in bed, their passion spent. It was a chilly night and the wedding ring patterned quilt was pulled tightly up to each of their chins. "Priss and I are going to Saturday Market tomorrow. I wish you could join us. Between your sleuthing and my move to the feminist law firm, I'm really missing alone time with you. Sometimes, I really miss the days when I was at Big Guy, Strong Man, Wimpy, and Dyke. I'm not complaining, just missing," April said. She kissed Morgan behind the ear. "Tell me all about your sleuthing today."

"I'm sorry if I'm neglecting you. I'm really caught up in this, I know." Morgan squeezed April's hand. "There were a lot of new developments. I just don't know what to make of most of them."

"Tell me about them."

Morgan smiled. "It always helps to talk to you, sweetheart." Morgan snuggled closer. "Sam found Judy's journal today."

"Where did he find it?"

"Between the mattress and box spring on her side of the bed. You know, where everybody hides things."

"Not very original. Did it tell you who the murderer is?"

"Maybe. It was kind of creepy reading the personal thoughts of a dead person."

"Morgan, I'm surprised at you. You read the personal thoughts of dead people all the time. Anaïs Nin, Sylvia Plath, Virginia Woolf."

"I mean the recently dead. It was full of unrequited love stuff. Like 'I love you so much, it hurts so much, I just want to die, but don't stop doin' it.'"

"Sounds like a line out of one of the poems you wrote me," April said. Morgan hit her with a pillow.

"Seriously, the diary was helpful because we now know she was suffering over someone, and I don't think it was her husband." Morgan retrieved the pillow and stuck it behind her back. "And whoever she was pining for was involved with another woman."

"Well, I would hope so! Aren't all of these club members married?"

"Yes, but of course we don't know that it's someone from the club that Judy was pining for. I just have a feeling it is. I also think the 'other woman' Judy was concerned about wasn't the guy's wife. But, who knows?"

"Really! These heterosexuals and their morals are beyond me." April snuggled up to Morgan, who tended to give off a lot of body heat. "Where does all of this leave David? Is he still in jail?"

"No. Even the district attorney acknowledges there's a strong connection between the two murders. There's the club, the shoes, and the fact that Judy had made those masks. David's free. I just hope he's still in therapy with someone besides Darrell Richardson.

"Of course, it's still possible we're looking for two killers. Judy's murder could have been opportunistic."

"You mean someone took advantage of Lucinda's death to knock off Judy for unrelated reasons?" Morgan nodded. "Who benefited from Judy's death?"

"Financially, her husband and daughter. Her will names both of them. But there's not really a lot of gain. They were up to their eyeballs in debt. The house hasn't accrued much equity. They took out a second mortgage to remodel the kitchen and turn the garage into Judy's studio. She had a small life insurance policy, which will probably just bury her if they're frugal with the funeral. And she had a nest egg of five thousand dollars in a personal account, which will go to her sixteen-year-old daughter."

"Was her daughter in serious need of money?"

"April!"

"Just joking." April tugged on Morgan's earlobe. "Did you find anything else?"

"Yeah. Judy was working on a series of masks of the club members. The only one that wasn't finished was of Lucinda's husband, Charlie, and someone had slashed it clear across the face."

"Do you think she was just taking a little artistic license?"

"Naw. The slashing felt really violent to me. I think it's connected to the murders."

"I wonder who will be next?"

"A chilling question." At that moment, there was an explosion of glass as a large rock came hurtling through one of the bedroom windows. April quickly leaped up and peered through the blinds.

"I saw a flash of a car driving away. I'm pretty sure it was white."

Morgan was examining the rock. A piece of paper was bound around it tightly with string. She picked up her pocketknife from the dresser to cut the string. In bold print, the note read, "I warned you once already." She showed it to April and reached for the phone.

Sam agreed to come right over. April swept up the glass fragments, while Morgan got cardboard and tape to keep out the winter air. It was several minutes before either of them spoke.

"Morgan, I'm really scared. This is getting a little too close to home."

"This is home, April. I'm feeling really violated." April grabbed Morgan, and they sat on the bed holding each other.

Morgan finally released her partner and said, "Let's get dressed. Sam will be here soon, and there's no telling who he'll bring with him. I'm not greeting Burly in my bathrobe."

When they were dressed, Morgan went to April's side of the bed and picked up the mattress.

"What are you doing?" April asked.

"Just checking."

29

Sam, Morgan, and Donald were in the kitchen Saturday morning. Sam had spent the night. Donald set a plate of puffy French toast in front of Sam. "Morgan, I made extra in case you change your mind. You know you'll be cranky all morning if you don't eat."

"I'll just have another cup of coffee, thanks."

"Okay, okay." Donald refilled her mug before he sat down to his own breakfast. Morgan stared glassy-eyed at her coffee.

"Morgan?" Sam's voice startled her. She jerked up. "You've been a great help to me on this case."

"Sure I have!" she said sarcastically. "I'd hate to think how far afield you'd be without me. Actually, you probably would have solved it by now if I weren't slowing you down."

"You sound angry."

"I am."

"I think you're really scared."

"I'm angry and scared."

"I think it's time for you to hang up your gumshoes and concentrate on the business of making people feel better."

"I don't make anyone feel anything!" Morgan glared at him

before relenting. "I'm sorry, Sam. These threats are getting to me. A rock through my bedroom window seems so much more personal than a letter at the office." She sipped her coffee. "But I don't want to let the bastard get the best of me. I'm not ready to quit."

"I thought you'd say that. So I've arranged," he paused and smiled at his lover, "to move in with Donald until this thing is settled."

Morgan laughed, "I appreciate the hardship on both of you."

"Always willing to do my part for law and order and the American way," Donald saluted her. "By the way," he added, "April and Priss are in the shower. They're going to Saturday Market and want you to join them. When you've all left, I'll replace that window."

"Thanks, Donald. I don't know what we'd do without you." She reached over and gave her "brother-in-law" a big smack on the cheek.

Morgan, April, and Priss were strolling the promenade along the river. "Oh, Priss. Look at the ducks!" A group of five mallards swam in a "v formation" close to the bank. Priss squatted down to see them better.

"Seymore! Can I have more bread?" Morgan dug half a loaf of French bread from Le Parrier out of her backpack. Priss tore the crusty bread into small pieces and threw them to the fowl.

"Are you scared, Morgan?" April asked while the ducks entertained Priss. "You seem pretty quiet today."

"I don't know if scared is the right word," Morgan ran her fingers through her brown curls. "I'm worried. I wonder what I've gotten you and Priss and Donald into."

"Looks like you've gotten Donald into love. I approve of that, and I approve of Sam."

"It seems they're very good for each other, although it's really too soon to tell."

"Yes. Give them ten years or so, and then we'll see." April put her arm around Morgan's shoulder. "But we're off topic. A rock through our bedroom window is not my idea of a good time. But I don't think you should be so intimidated that you give up working with Sam. You seem to have a real passion for this."

"It would be terribly hard to stop, but I would if you wanted me to."

"Oh, no. I'm not making this decision for you. You know me better than that!" April squeezed Morgan's shoulder hard.

"Ow!"

"Quack, quack, quack!" said Priss. She had noticed that she'd lost her moms' full attention and came running up. "Can I take a duckie home? Please? I'll feed it and everything."

Charles Frazier sat behind his desk in his office at the head-quarters of Hawthorne Business Machines. Sam and Morgan were in matching leather side chairs facing him. There was a picture of Randolph on the wall. It was probably from high school, Morgan thought. He looked a couple of years younger and a couple of years less angry.

"Do you always work Saturday mornings, Mr. Frazier?" Sam asked.

"I think since we're getting to know each other so well, you can call me Charlie, Sam." Charlie included Morgan with a warm smile. "Not always, but I often work weekends. It pays to stay ahead. It seems the two of you must feel the same way."

"Why didn't you tell us about the Chandelier Club, Charlie?"

Charlie looked down and slowly shook his head. "I was hoping that business wouldn't come up. It all seemed harmless enough. But now, with Judy and Lucinda both dead, I just don't know." Charlie pulled at the knot of his maroon tie. He stopped and looked up at Sam.

"What was your relationship with Judy Wharton?"

"I'll be as frank with you as I can, Sam. I think the woman had a special feeling for me." Charlie seemed pleased. "She never said as much, of course. It would have been really awkward, Paul being a friend and all. It was just an impression I got."

"How'd you feel about her?" Morgan asked.

"Fine woman. Very passionate. The artist in her, I guess. But if you mean, did I have a special feeling for her? No. Lucinda was probably the only woman for me." Charlie looked down again, and Morgan noticed there were tears in his eyes.

"Why did you and Lucinda break up?" Morgan asked.

"I don't know exactly. She never forgave me for moving out here. She had really carved out a niche for herself in Boston. It was hard on her, starting over again. I'm a few years older than Lucinda, but I think I'm a little more flexible. I looked on the move as an adventure. Besides, I'm from here originally. I was glad for the transfer." Charlie patted his hair.

"Of course, that wasn't all of it," Charlie continued. "We just seemed to drift further and further apart. It got so we couldn't talk about anything without it ending in an argument. I wanted to go for couple's counseling, but Lucinda wouldn't hear of it. I don't think she really trusted therapists, except maybe Richardson, but of course, he was her supervisor. So seeing him was out."

Charlie stared out the window for a minute before continuing. "I thought we were one of those couples who were in for the long haul. Twenty-three years is a long time. The separation was bad enough, but her death, too . . . " Charlie shook his head.

"Tell us about your first wife's death," said Sam abruptly.

Morgan thought the man stopped breathing. "It has nothing to do with this mess. Ginny died in a tragic accident. We were very happily married. She was a devoted bird-watcher, and she often went on outings." Charlie paused to catch his breath. "She went on an Audubon Society field trip looking for tufted puffins off Cape Arago. That was when we lived here. It was early in the morning and very foggy when she slipped on the steep trail and fell to her death."

"Did anyone see her fall?"

"Yes. She and another person were a ways behind the group. They had spotted a flock of common murres who were teaching their fledglings to fly by pushing them off a seastack. The fellow was very broken up about Ginny's death."

"What was his name?"

"I'm sorry. I don't recall."

"Did you know Judy Wharton made a mask of you?" Sam asked.

"Oh, yes. She made a plaster mold right on my face. Messy stuff. She did one of Lucinda first. I wonder where it is now?"

"Where were you between two and six on Thursday afternoon?"

"Right here in the office. My secretary was here, too."

"She didn't leave until six?"

"Well, actually no." Charlie shifted in his chair.

"Do you have any enemies, Charlie?"

"Who me? No, I can't think of anyone who's angry with me. Besides Lucinda, that is."

30

Leaving Charlie's office, Sam said, "I scheduled another interview for us while you were getting dressed this morning." Morgan looked at him. "I didn't mention it before because you were having such a bad morning." Sam started the car. "You don't have to go. I can drop you off first."

"Huh? Oh, I get it. I knew we'd have to talk to her again. I'm going. You're not leaving me out at this point."

"Good girl." Sam gave Morgan's left hand a squeeze.

Morgan glared at him. "Don't patronize me."

"Sorry. We're meeting Maude at her office. She said she didn't want us to upset Jeffrey."

Morgan rolled her eyes. She gave Sam directions, and soon they pulled into the parking lot beside the huge Victorian mansion that housed Maude's office. Her red Jaguar was the only other car in the lot.

Morgan was overwhelmed by the decor. She knew Maude had hired an expensive New York firm to decorate the space but she still thought it gaudy. Abstract paintings by a famous artist, with bold slashes of purple, blue, and red, hung on the mauve walls.

As pretentious as her office, Maude was wearing a peacock blue ensemble with wide, straight-legged trousers and a matching knee-length tunic belted with numerous strands of raw silk in reds and purples. Cherry red boots completed her outfit. She made an overpowering picture posed in her purple velvet, high-backed chair.

"Hello, Detective. Morgan. I've just been sitting here meditating, awaiting your arrival." Her arms lay along those of the chair. Each hand was palm-up and cupped. "Please be seated." Sam and Morgan obeyed.

"We have a few more questions to ask you, Dr. Ross," Sam said.

"Yes. Poor Judy. Poor Lucinda. Poor people."

"Do you have any idea who killed them?"

"You think the same person killed them both?"

"Dr. Ross, I'll ask the questions. You provide the answers."

Uh-oh, thought Morgan. He won't get anything out of her now.

"Answer the question, please," Sam said after thirty seconds of silence.

"That would be the question you asked me before I asked my question and before you so rudely reprimanded me. Is that correct, Sergeant? Oh, dear, that's another question, isn't it?"

Sam was steaming. Morgan decided to try. "Maude, we really need your help. Obviously, there's at least one killer on the loose. And if he has killed twice, there's no telling when he may kill again. Or who. It could even be another woman in the club: Norma Bates, Corky, or you. The murderer may be someone you know. Please help us."

"Of course, Morgan. That's why I'm here this morning." Maude crossed her legs and settled into the familiar role of helper. "It's hard for me to imagine that anyone in the club could be responsible. Certainly, neither Walter nor I had anything to do with any of this. Corky's a flake, but she's not a killer. And someone of Darrell Richardson's reputation is not going to stoop to murder.

"Norma Bates is depressive but basically harmless. Collin Bates is rather rigid. That leaves Charlie or Paul or both. Aren't spouses the most likely suspects?" Maude looked at Sam. "Never mind. I'll answer that myself. I think they are. Although it's hard to imagine Charlie killing Lucinda. I think he was still carrying a torch for her. Paul and Judy were having their problems. I told you about that last time we talked. But I don't think Paul would kill his wife."

"After we talked with you on Wednesday, did you speak with Judy Wharton?" Sam asked.

"Yes. I called her that afternoon and told her you would be interviewing her."

"Why?"

"She was a friend of mine."

"That may have cost your friend her life."

"What do you mean?"

"Maybe the murderer didn't want us to talk to Judy." Sam sat forward in his chair. "Where were you between two and six on Thursday?"

"Here. Seeing clients. Naturally, I can't violate confidentiality and give you their names without a court order. But my secretary was here the whole time, and I don't have a back door."

"Why didn't you tell us Judy had made a mask of you?" Morgan asked.

"Oh, I didn't think it was important. I wonder if Paul would let me have it? I think it would be perfect for my waiting room."

31

Sam and Morgan were sitting under a big leaf maple in the Arboretum picnicking on avocado-and-sprout sandwiches from Veggie's takeout.

"I've got the printout of the background checks I ran on the club members," Sam said. "Not too much here. Collin Bates was arrested once for practicing without a license after the medical board jerked it for malpractice. That was in Maryland, seven years ago. But a judge reinstated his license, and the charges were dropped."

"Didn't you say whoever killed Judy either got lucky or knew what he was doing? Because of the placement of the knife? A doctor, even a dermatologist, would know what he was doing."

"You're right. We should interview him again." Sam shifted around on the tarp that protected them from the damp ground. "The only other one with a criminal record will surprise you."

"Maude?"

"Only in your dreams, sweetie. But you're close. Walter Gibbons."

"Really?"

"Yes. He's been arrested twice. Both times in raids on gay bars in New York. 1967 and '68."

"Pre-Stonewall. I didn't know about Walter. I wonder if Maude does."

"Maybe they're both bisexual."

"According to Norma Bates, the club certainly isn't." Morgan slurped her latté. "I'd like to go over all the romantic liaisons of the club members. Perhaps something new will occur to us."

"Go on." Sam unwrapped his carob brownie.

"Well, Maude is having an affair with Lance Rogers. But, he's not a club member. Paul had the hots for Lucinda, but she didn't reciprocate. Instead, she slept with a client. Judy was having an affair, but we don't know with whom. Charlie thinks Judy had a crush on him, but who knows?"

"Who knows, indeed. It's all too messy."

"You know, only one person was a suspect before we learned about the club, and, still is."

"Charlie Frazier." Sam looked longingly at the second brownie. Morgan handed it to him. "And don't you think Charlie is connected with Judy's murder through the mask?"

"I don't know. Could be," Sam replied.

Morgan was throwing the crusts from her sandwich to three hungry sparrows. "Let's assume you're right, women don't strangle and stab people to death. And let's assume the killer is a member of the club. That means it's Paul, Charlie, Collin, Darrell, or Walter."

"Two of the five are now widowers," Sam observed.

"Do you suppose this is something like *Stepford Wives*?"

"Huh?"

"It was a book and then a television movie. The husbands all belonged to a club. They killed their wives and replaced them with lifelike robots."

"And maybe Judy was in on the plot. That's why she made the masks. They had to kill her because she knew too much. Do you subscribe to the Kennedy assassination conspiracy, too?"

"Yes." Morgan picked up the remains of their lunch and

deposited them in a nearby trash can shaped like an owl. "I suppose we should go see Collin Bates again."

"And since it's Saturday, bet we'll find him at Columbia-Edgewater Greens."

✳ ✳ ✳

They caught up with Collin on the thirteenth green and waited patiently through four putts before the ball rolled into the cup with a satisfying thunk.

"Ruined my concentration," Bates complained as he joined them on a nearby bench. He took a white hanky from his back pocket and dabbed his temples. Morgan wondered if he was sweating from the exertion of the game or from nerves. She also wondered if Norma had knitted the pink-and-blue-tasseled booties that covered Collin's clubs. "I suppose this interruption has to do with Judy Wharton's death."

"That's right," Sam answered. "Did you know Judy outside of the club?"

Collin's pale skin got even paler. "I don't want Norma to know about this. She wouldn't understand. Judy and I met for lunch twice. Nothing else. Just lunch. I know what you're thinking." Collin looked at Morgan.

No, you don't, Morgan thought.

Collin was still talking, "We seemed to be kindred souls. We liked discussing art, music, the theater. It was completely innocent, but Norma would never understand, and I don't want to upset her."

"When did you last see Judy?" Sam asked.

"At the last club meeting. Before Lucinda's death."

"Where were you on Thursday between two and six?"

"I was at my office until five. Norma picked me up there, and we went to an early movie."

"How well do you know Paul Wharton?"

"Just through the club. Darrell Richardson invited us to join originally. We know each other from med school." Collin wiped his face again. "Officer Reynolds, first Lucinda and then Judy.

This thing has me worried. Do you think I should take Norma away for awhile just so she's safe?"

"Don't leave town," Sam said flatly.

32

Saturday night, after everyone had polished off Sorrowful but Sweet Rain Soup, Two-Thousand-Year-Old Turtle Egg in Nest, Seven Mysteries Noodles, and Bamboo Palace Moo Gai, Morgan cracked open her fortune cookie, unfolded the white paper, and read, "You will find what you are looking for."

"Mine says, 'Love is at hand,'" said Donald, reaching out to take Sam's hand. "What's yours say, Sam?"

"'Confucius say: Wise man leaves no trail,'" read Sam.

"Fortunately, we're not looking for a wise man," said Morgan.

"Read mine! Read mine!" Priss held her fortune up to April.

"It says: 'Bedtime for little girls.'"

"No, it doesn't!" Priss's face turned into a pout.

"I'm sorry, sweetie," April gave her daughter a squeeze. "I was teasing you. It really says: 'Life is full of wonders to the wondering eye.'"

"What does that mean?" Priss wanted to know.

"I'm not sure," began April. "I guess it means it's good to be curious. And you certainly are a Curious George. And you know what?"

"What?" Priss leaned forward, her face supported in her hands.

"It really is time for bed."

"Oh, Mommy!" In spite of her protest, Priss made the rounds kissing everyone good night and let April lead her by the hand out of the kitchen.

"April didn't share her fortune," Morgan said, picking up the scrap of paper on April's plate. "Uh-oh. It says: 'Trouble is at your door.'"

"Not a very nice fortune," remarked Sam. "I think they ought to stick to three basic messages: 'You will meet a handsome stranger,' 'You will have great success,' and 'Good news is on its way.'" Donald pressed his hand. Sam continued, "By the way, Perry called while you and April were getting the food, Morgan. He spent some time with Judy's daughter, Valerie, this afternoon going through her mom's closet. She told him that a pair of Judy's shoes are missing. A pair of red Birkenstocks she always wore around the house."

"She probably had them on when she was murdered," surmised Morgan. "So we're looking for gray suede pumps and red sandals." She started picking up plates and silverware. "You know, there was something very strange about Judy Wharton."

"What?" asked Sam, as he gathered together the white paper cartons.

"Her house. Except for her studio, it didn't look like the house of an artist. It was too neat. Too 'decorated.' All that white on white. Too *Architectural Digest.*"

"You're right," Sam said. "Let's ask Paul about it. The funeral's tomorrow. I have to go. You want to come?"

"No. I want to be a mommy and lover tomorrow. Maybe not in that order."

33

Monday, Morgan left her office to meet Victoria for lunch. She stepped out into a rainy but not raining day, strolling to the end of the block, where she waited for the walk signal before crossing. Halfway across, a dark car swerved in front of her. A guy leaned out the window with an object in his hand and said, "Gotcha."

Morgan stopped cold, waiting for the bullet to pierce her body. Instead, a stream of water hit her full in the face. The sound of adolescent laughter filled her ears as the car sped away. Morgan continued across the street on weak knees. Her heart was still pounding when she arrived at Victoria's office.

※ ※ ※

"Hello, Dr. McRain." Mrs. Hatfield smiled at her.

"Oh, hello," Morgan responded, trying to recover her equilibrium. "I'm here to see Victoria Trimbell."

"Do you have an appointment, dear?"

"Victoria and I are lunching together. I understand she's quite happy with this new office arrangement." Mrs. Hatfield smiled. "I was wondering what it's like to work with Dr. Richardson."

"Dr. Richardson is a wonderful man and a very competent psychiatrist. He helps so many people. Now, if you will excuse me, I need to make some copies." She stood up but before leaving the room, said, "I'm certain Dr. Trimbell will be with you soon."

Darrell Richardson walked into the room. "Hi," said Morgan. "I was just talking about you with Mrs. Hatfield. She had some interesting things to say," Morgan lied. "By the way, how well did you know Judy Wharton?"

"I don't think this is an appropriate time or place, Dr. McRain."

"Would you rather I came back with Detective Reynolds?"

"Let's just keep this brief," Richardson replied stiffly. "I didn't know her well. I admired her art. I think she was quite talented." He placed the thumb of his left hand underneath his cheek bone and the forefinger across his upper lip as he spoke. "Her death is certainly a tragedy."

"Where were you between two and six on Thursday afternoon?"

"Right here. In my office. Let's see," he reached for a large appointment book on Mrs. Hatfield's desk and flipped back a couple of pages. "Yes. I had clients at one and two, a break at three, and clients again at four and five."

"And during your break?"

"I stayed at my desk and did paperwork." Mrs. Hatfield, who had come back into the room, was nodding her head.

Victoria walked into the room. "Hi, Morgan. Darrell, Morgan and I are having lunch. Do you want to join us?"

"No, no, that's quite all right. I have another commitment."

Over lunch, Morgan told Victoria all about the rock coming through the bedroom window.

"How's April handling it?" Victoria wanted to know.

"She seems perfectly cool about the whole thing. You know April, it takes a lot to ruffle her feathers." Morgan took a bite of her salad. "I'm trying to be as calm, but I don't think I'm succeeding. On the way to your office, a kid shot me with a squirt gun, and I thought it was time to cash in my chips." Morgan paused for another bite.

"I'm really concerned about you," Vic took her friend's hand. "Don't you think you're in over your head? If I were April, I'd order you to leave this detecting stuff alone."

"Vic, I appreciate your concern, but you should know that April doesn't order me to do anything, except maybe in intimate moments."

34

"I'm sorry to have to disturb you, Mr. Wharton, right after the funeral and all," said Sam on Monday evening. "But solving Judy's murder can't wait. We need to ask you a few more questions. This won't take long." Sam settled himself on one of the white sofas next to Morgan and across from Paul.

"In your wife's studio we found a mask of Charlie Frazier," Sam paused.

"Yes. As I told you before, she was working on masks of everyone in the club," said Paul.

"Do you know why Charlie's was the last mask she was making?" Sam asked.

"No. I never thought about the order. In fact, I haven't actually seen any of the masks. I rarely go into Judy's studio. When she did the mold of my face, she had the other masks covered up. Judy doesn't like anyone to see her work in progress."

"When was the last time you were in the studio?" asked Sam.

"The night she did the casting of me. That must have been about a week ago."

"You haven't seen any of the masks hanging on the wall?"

Morgan asked. Paul shook his head. "There was an interesting arrangement to the masks." Morgan looked at Sam, who nodded. She continued, "They were arranged in pairs by married couples, except you and Lucinda were together." Paul hung his head. "Judy's mask hung alone, and Charlie's was still on her worktable. But Charlie's . . . " Morgan paused, and Paul looked up expectantly. Morgan continued, " . . . was slit from brow to lip by a big knife."

"The same knife that killed Judy?" Paul asked.

"No," answered Sam. "But it was from the same set in your kitchen. We found it in a neighbor's garbage can. Wiped clean of prints. What do you make of this?"

"I have no idea," said Paul. "I guess someone had it in for both Judy and Charlie. But I have no idea who."

"Charlie thinks Judy was interested in him," Morgan said.

"Really?" said Paul. "I didn't know anything about that. If it's true, I wish I had known."

"Why?" asked Morgan.

Paul looked at her directly and said, "Then I wouldn't have felt so guilty about my feelings for Lucinda. And maybe the four of us could have worked something out."

"We found Judy's diary," Sam said.

Paul's face showed no reaction. "What diary?" he asked.

"You didn't know your wife kept a diary?"

"No."

"She seemed to have been writing about a lover. Do you know who that could be?"

"No!"

"You sound jealous," commented Morgan.

"No. Just surprised. I guess I thought I would know if Judy had a lover. I really don't have any idea who it could be."

Morgan was surveying the living room and remembering what bothered her about it. "Who decorated your house?" she asked Paul abruptly.

Paul frowned. "What? Oh, I did. It's sort of a hobby of mine. I might have gone into interior design if I hadn't been interested in law."

"Judy was okay with you doing the decorating?"

"Of course. If I had left it up to her, the whole place would probably look like her studio. You saw what a mess that is!" Morgan looked around again at the sterile room and decided she preferred Judy's homey studio, even with its clay dust.

"Let's go back to your alibi for the time of Judy's death," said Sam.

"Uh, actually, I'm glad you brought that up." Paul frowned again. "To tell the truth, I didn't go to Pioneer Place. I was with Corky Vanderpelt."

35

"There must be a clue somewhere," Morgan mused over her peanut-butter-and-jelly omelet on Tuesday morning.

"I wish I could help, but I gotta go. See you all tonight." April stood and kissed Morgan and Priss on the tops of their heads. Her lips brushed Donald's cheek as she passed by.

"Bye, April," Donald called as she swooped out of the room. "Don't be late tonight. I'm making Indonesian curry." Donald slid another omelet onto a plate and placed it on the table. "I wonder what's holding Sam up?"

As if on cue, Sam strolled into the kitchen straightening the knot on his paisley tie, which he was wearing over a blue denim work shirt. "Hmmm. Something smells good."

"It's peanut butter and jelly," said Priss.

"No, thanks. I'll just have eggs."

"That's your plate on the table," Donald winked at Priss. "Want some more coffee, Morgan?"

"Yes, but I'll get it. You finish your own omelet." Morgan picked up the white vacuum carafe from its stand and filled the red mug at Sam's place. "Do you want anything while I'm up, Priss?"

The child thrust out her sippy cup.

"Use words, and make sure one of them is 'please.'"

"More orange juice, puleeeze."

"I think we'd better go see your friend Corky after you finish with clients tonight," said Sam. He looked up to see Donald glaring at him. "Make that after dinner."

"Okay, I can manage that. What are you working on today?"

Sam put down his coffee mug. "I just got off the phone with Perry." Sam cut into his omelet with his fork. "I'm going to have a little chat with Dr. Bates today. Quite a coincidence his being Victoria's dermatologist."

"Indeed," said Morgan. "Sometimes Portland seems like a small town." Sam put the first forkful into his mouth. "What the hell! It is peanut butter!" He continued chewing. "This is delicious! Crabapple jelly?"

"Yes," said Donald, sitting down at the table. "I made it myself."

"I'm a very happy man," said Sam, giving Donald a smile. "Now if I could only be a successful detective."

❋ ❋ ❋

"So what did you find out from Collin Bates?" Morgan asked as she and Sam were on their way to Corky and Darrell's house.

"Not much. He couldn't seem to remember who Victoria was. Looked up his records. He's seen her twice. Once last week, as I knew, and another time six months ago when she had a heat rash."

"I know we're going to question Corky about her relationship with Paul," said Morgan. "But what are we going to ask Darrell?"

Sam laughed. "I know you think you covered everything in your interview with him yesterday. But I don't think it will hurt to ask him a few more questions."

They found the address they were looking for. It was a large chrome-and-glass house that hung over the west hills. Corky opened the door on the second ring wearing a hot pink, silk lounging outfit. She led them into a spacious living room, one wall of which was all glass, giving spectacular views of the city lights below.

Darrell Richardson strolled into the room wearing a smoking jacket over slacks. Morgan felt like they were at a slumber party. She looked around for the Cokes and popcorn.

"To what do we owe the pleasure, Detective?" asked Richardson, who remained standing.

"Dr. McRain and I have a few more questions to ask you and your wife, Dr. Richardson."

"I fail to understand Dr. McRain's role in this inquiry, Detective Reynolds."

"It's very simple. The police department has hired Dr. McRain as a consultant especially for this investigation," said Sam. "Now, if you have no further objections, perhaps we could get to our questions."

"I'm not sure I have anything to add to what I've already told you," said Richardson.

Sam turned to Corky. "How long have you been sleeping with Paul Wharton?"

"The club has been in existence . . . "

"I don't mean at club meetings. How long have you been having an affair with Paul Wharton?"

"What? This is preposterous!" said Darrell.

"I'm waiting for an answer, Dr. Vanderpelt-Richardson," said Sam. "We've already talked with Paul."

"That bastard!" said Corky. "I've been comforting him. He was very upset over Lucinda's death, and I don't think Judy realized how hard it was for him. And then, she was killed. Poor man. But he had no right telling you. I'm going to kill him!" Corky looked around in the silence that followed her outburst. "That was just a figure of speech. I didn't mean it."

Darrell sat, looking more beaten than angry, Morgan thought. "Judy Wharton was having an affair with somebody. Do either of you know who it was?" asked Morgan.

"Everyone seems to be sleeping with someone else's

spouse," said Darrell quietly. "But as to whom specifically Judy was seeing, I don't know."

"Don't look at me," said Corky.

36

Morgan was playing leapfrog with Corky and Darrell and Walter. As they played, the others turned into pink bunnies and started to do what bunnies do best. They were joined by Maude and Collin and Norma and Lucinda and Charlie and Paul and Judy. Morgan watched, feeling fascinated and horrified. She was holding April's hand. She turned to look into April's eyes, but as she looked, April's skin crumbled away, and she saw only skull.

A ringing sound filled her ears. Gratefully, she opened her eyes and glanced at the clock before picking up the phone. Three-fifteen Wednesday morning. "Hello?" Morgan said sleepily.

"Morgan McRain, please," said a male voice.

"This is she."

"I'm Dr. Landaur calling from the intensive care unit of Emmanuel Hospital. Your mother is here. She's suffered a coronary arrest. I suggest you come immediately."

Morgan was wide awake. "Is she okay?"

"I'd rather discuss her condition with you in person. Just ask for me at reception in the intensive care unit."

"April?" Morgan shook her partner's sleeping body gently.

"Huh?"

"April. It's my mother. She's had a heart attack."

"Oh, no! Oh, Morgan, I'm sorry." April propped herself up on one elbow and looked at Morgan, who was already moving around the bedroom collecting shoes, socks, etc. "Where is she?"

"Emmanuel Hospital," Morgan put one foot through a pair of jeans. "A doctor from there just called me. I've got to hurry. He wouldn't tell me how she is, so I think it's bad."

"I'll come with you." April pulled back the covers and sat up.

"No. Don't. You have that trial in the morning. You need to be fresh." Morgan was buttoning a shirt. She had to start over because the buttons didn't come out even. "I have no idea how long this will take, and since today is my day off, I can come back and nap, and you can't." She thrust her arms into a sweatshirt. "I'll call you as soon as I know anything."

"Promise?"

"Yes," Morgan kissed her softly on the lips. "Go back to sleep."

Morgan grabbed a parka and her keys. She pressed the garage door opener, hoping the door's rumbling wouldn't wake up Donald and Sam. She carefully backed the yellow Previa out of the garage and headed for the freeway.

I just talked to her Monday morning, she thought. I really should call her more often. I wonder if she wasn't feeling well and just wouldn't say. She hates to worry me. This is just the way Dad went. I hope I'm not too late.

Morgan was pulling off the exit, aware that she couldn't remember a single thing about the drive. I already have her dead and buried, she thought. I must try to stay in the present moment.

She easily found a parking place in the big emergency lot. She set the parking brake, pulled out her keys, and opened the door of the van. As she reached back in to pick up her purse from the passenger seat, someone grabbed her from behind and pushed her to the ground. Her nose was grinding into the pavement. Her arms were pinned behind her painfully, and a knee was pressing into her kidneys.

Hot breath was in her ear. She realized that her hands were being tied with what felt like a leather belt. This is probably good, she thought. If he were going to kill me, he wouldn't bother tying me up. In spite of all the pain, her mind felt crystal clear and calm. "What do you want?" she asked.

The response was a blow to the right side of her head. She heard a hoarse whisper, "Shut up. Don't make another sound or I'll kill you. You haven't taken my warnings seriously. I want to make sure you remember this." He pulled her head up by her hair, but before she could see anything, he slugged her directly in the face. Blood spurted everywhere.

Morgan felt strangely detached. I'm glad I have on old clothes, she thought. I wonder if my nose is broken.

Breathing in her ear again. "Stop playing detective. It's not a game. This is your last warning." For emphasis, he bit through her earlobe. "Your mother is dead." She passed out.

Morgan had a headache. Not just in her forehead but all over her head. Both sides hurt. The back hurt. Her face hurt. Her hands were numb. Her feet were cold. Terrible dream. No dream. "Mother!" she screamed.

She opened her eyes. Actually, only one eye. The other one wouldn't open. Her hands were no longer bound, but they still had no feeling. Nevertheless, she used them to push herself up. Her shoes were missing. Her black loafers. She looked around. The sky seemed a little lighter. No shoes. The van door was still open. Her purse was still in the passenger seat. She picked it up.

Keys. Morgan checked her pockets. No keys. She looked around on the pavement again. Each time she bent over, her head throbbed and she felt dizzy. She gave up and made her way toward the entrance that said EMERGENCY in blue lights. It seemed appropriate.

Morgan stood a long time at the reception desk before a woman in a nurse's uniform looked up from a computer monitor. "Name. Last name first. Insurance company."

"I'm here to see my mother. She's in the intensive care unit. Could you direct me?"

"Visiting hours are from two to four in the afternoon."

"You don't understand. She's had a heart attack. Dr. Landaur asked me to come. Where can I find him?"

"How do you spell that name?"

"I don't really know. Try L-A-N-D-A-U-R."

The woman pushed some buttons on the computer terminal. "There's no doctor here by that name."

"Good grief! Try a different spelling!"

"The computer has already done that. What's your mother's name?"

"Lillian McRain. I'm sorry. McRain, Lillian."

The woman glanced at Morgan. "There's no one in this hospital by that name."

"Check the morgue," Morgan said quietly.

"I already did," the woman stared at Morgan. "I think it's broken."

"The computer?"

"Your nose."

"Can I use the phone?"

"Pay phone. Down the hall to your right. And I might as well check you into the emergency room. Leave your insurance information with me."

Morgan fumbled around in the purse dangling from her shoulder. She pulled her Blue Cross card out of her wallet and plunked it on the counter. She felt around in her change purse for a quarter as she hurried to the phone.

"Hello?" answered a sleepy voice.

"Mom, is that you? Are you all right?"

"Who else would it be, Morgan? You dialed my number, didn't you? What are you doing calling me in the middle of the night? Like to scare me half to death! Now if you can't sleep, try warm milk." Morgan remembered why she didn't call her mother more often. The next call was to April.

37

"Morgan, is that you?" April's voice had a hysterical edge to it.

"Who else?" answered the bandage-wrapped skull. "Don't worry. It's not as bad as it looks."

"It looks god-awful," said Sam at April's side. "How are you feeling?"

"Like I have a broken nose and a pierced earlobe and a black eye," said Morgan. "Other than that, swell." Morgan tried to sit up but immediately felt dizzy and lay back down on the cot.

"Did you get a look at the bastard?" asked Sam.

"No. I never really saw him," answered Morgan. "And I didn't recognize his voice, either over the phone or in person. Of course, he whispered in person. But there was something about how he smelled that was familiar. I just can't put my finger on it."

"Don't try to think too hard right now, honey," April said as she took hold of Morgan's hand and squeezed it.

"Was it an aftershave lotion or body odor or . . . " Sam stopped when he noticed April's reproving glare.

"I just can't seem to remember what it was," said Morgan. "It's right around the corner of my mind, if you know what I mean."

"Maybe going over the whole event, step by step, will help," said Sam, quickly adding, "When you're ready, of course."

The curtain surrounding Morgan's bed in the emergency room was pulled back, and a woman in a white coat came into the area, smiling warmly. "You're well enough to hold court, I see."

"Dr. Kauffman, this is my partner, April Daley, and my friend, Sam Reynolds. Sam is a detective with the Portland Police."

"Pleased to meet you both," said Dr. Kauffman. "I bet you're wondering when you can go home," she said to Morgan. "Well, the answer is any time. It's important to stay quiet for the rest of the day." Dr. Kauffman raised Morgan's eyelids one at a time and stuck a scope in each ear canal as she talked. "I've written a prescription for some pain pills. You'll probably feel even worse tomorrow than you do today. Make an appointment with your regular physician to take a look at you in about a week. Any questions?"

"Do you think I can make it in the world on charm alone?"

"No," answered the gray-haired physician. "But when you're all healed up, you'll only notice a slight bump on your nose. And twice a day I want you to wash that lobe on both sides with hydrogen peroxide. Human bites are the worst for infections."

Dr. Kauffman left, and April bent down and kissed Morgan's bandaged nose lightly. "Your poor little proboscis!"

"Yeah," Morgan stuck out her lower lip. "And to think some people thought it was too big before this!"

"Only the killer thought that, Morgan, and I think he was reminding you of it this morning." Sam sat at the foot of Morgan's bed. "Obviously, he was familiar enough with this hospital's emergency parking lot to know it would be practically deserted that time of morning. My men couldn't find any witnesses. One of the guys talked to a couple in a Volkswagen camper bus who spent the night here. They're traveling and said they usually seek out hospital parking lots to sleep in because they're generally very quiet if you can sleep through the occasional siren. They didn't hear a thing last night."

"None of the club members live in this part of town," said Morgan.

"You're right, they don't. But Charlie's office is near here. Not only that, I ran a check while you were getting patched up and confirmed that both Darrell Richardson and Collin Bates have hospital privileges here."

"And I suppose Walter Gibbons and Paul Wharton have recently been visiting sick relatives here as well," Morgan's voice was sarcastic.

"I guess I could check that out," Sam was tentative.

"You work on that, Sam, while I help Morgan get dressed, and we'll meet you by the front door in fifteen minutes," April was being efficient.

Morgan watched April take items of clothing out of an overnight bag she had brought with her. Panties, bra, sweatshirt, chinos, socks, and a pair of Nikes. April surveyed the clothing. "I don't think that sweatshirt will go over your head easily. Here, I'll trade with you." April unbuttoned the yellow long-sleeved oxford she was wearing and pulled it off. She quickly yanked the sweatshirt over her bare chest.

"You brought me a bra, but you didn't bother to put one on yourself?" Morgan teased.

"I wasn't thinking about me, I was thinking about you," April said defensively. "I didn't even bother with socks." She held up one bare ankle for Morgan to see. "Why aren't you getting dressed? Do you need help?"

"Probably. But that isn't what I'm concerned about right now. Come here." Morgan pulled April to her, tight. April was stiff, then Morgan felt her body relax followed by a splash of tears on her cheek. April's body trembled with sobs. Morgan held her for two or three minutes until the shaking stopped, and April found her voice.

"I should be comforting you."

"April, I'm really sorry. I should never have gotten involved in this. I know I've scared you, and I've really scared myself, too. I love you so much. I never want to cause you pain."

April sobbed loudly. "After you called, I just kept seeing you lying in that parking lot. He could have killed you!"

"I know. I'm a little puzzled that he didn't."

April pulled back a moment and looked into Morgan's good eye. "What would I have done if he had? What would Priss have done?" Morgan pulled her close again.

Just then Big Nurse from *One Flew Over the Cuckoo's Nest* pulled back the curtain. Morgan hurriedly dressed.

Morgan was propped up in bed with lots of pillows. April had left for court. Sam was out investigating. Donald and Priss were in the kitchen finger painting. Morgan was bored. Her head hurt too much for reading or television. She had tried napping but felt too wired. She tried to think through the case, but her head hurt worse with the effort. As a last resort, she was trying to conjure a sexual fantasy of a big, domineering butch, but she couldn't quite pull it off. The phone rang. Shortly, Donald was in the room.

"I tried to tell her you weren't up to talking to anyone, but she insisted."

"Who?"

"Maude Ross."

"Do me a favor, and check my horoscope for today," Morgan sighed. "Oh well, I think I'd rather get it over with than dread talking to her later." She picked up the receiver, "Hello, Maude."

"Morgan, your houseboy told me you were a little under the weather, but this is important. I need to talk to your detective."

"He's not my detective. Call Central Precinct, and ask for Sam Reynolds."

"I already did, and they said he's in the field, whatever that means. I've got to talk to him."

"When I see him, I'll tell him you called."

"Oh, I might as well tell you since you're mixed up in this nasty business. Walter didn't come home last night. It's just not like him at all. I've called everywhere, but I can't find him. Do you think he could have been killed?"

38

"Morgan? Morgan? Are you there?"

"Stay put, Maude." Morgan pushed the off button on the phone before Maude could say another word. She called Sam's car phone. "Sam, it's me," she said when he answered. "Something's come up. Please come to the house as soon as you can."

"What is it, Morgan?"

"I'll tell you when you get here."

"Tell me now."

"No. If I do, you'll just leave me out, and it's too late for that. Besides, I'm bored and I can't read and I can't sleep . . . "

"I was on my way there anyway."

Morgan knew she was being difficult, but she didn't care. Someone had beat her up; she was entitled to a little moodiness. She climbed out of bed and opened her closet door. There had been entirely too much dressing and undressing today. She sighed and pulled on a pair of gray wool slacks, a blue shirt, and a lambswool cardigan. She looked for her black loafers before remembering she no longer possessed them. She shuddered to think about what use they had been put to today.

She slipped her feet into a pair of blue moccasins and

turned to the full-length mirror to survey her appearance. From her neck down, she looked quite presentable. From her neck up, she was a mess. "All the better to see you, my dear," she said in her best big-bad-wolf voice.

She left a brief note for Donald propped on her pillows and snuck down the stairs. She heard Priss's and Donald's voices coming from the kitchen as she eased the front door open. Sam pulled up within a couple of minutes. She got in on the passenger side before telling him, "We need to go see Maude Ross. Walter has disappeared."

"You need to get back in bed. Do you know how you look?"

"Too casual? Think I should have dressed more formally?"

"You know what I mean. Besides, I can handle Maude Ross."

"I'm not so sure. Anyway, Donald said an outing would be good for me," Morgan lied. "Maude's at her office. Turn right at the corner . . ."

"I remember how to get there," Sam shook his head and eased the little car into first gear. "Look, Morgan. This is my job. This is what I do every day to earn a living. I know I involved you in the beginning because of your expertise . . ."

"And to meet Donald."

Sam grimaced. "But now that this has happened, I think it's time for you to back out. Actually, I thought so when the rock was thrown through your bedroom window. I should have insisted then."

"I didn't want to stop then, and I don't want to now. I'm not really sure why I've gotten so caught up in this. Finding Lucinda's body certainly involved me right away." Morgan ran a hand through her thick curls. "But more than that, it's that . . . well, it's hard to explain. I came along after my parents had stopped thinking about children and had settled down to making each other miserable. Most of my childhood was spent in a cold war. They didn't talk to each other, and they didn't talk to me except to transmit messages, 'Morgan, tell your father his brother is on the phone.' 'Morgan, tell your mother to pass the salt.'

"I guess that's why I became a therapist. I wanted someone

to talk to me. And I've always liked hearing secrets. My parents never let me know what was going on. When I was five my mother got me up early one morning, told me to get dressed, drove me to a big brick building, and took me into a room with a whole lot of kids. A tall woman told me to sit down. That was my introduction to school. I was so overwhelmed that within a few days the teacher reported to my mother that I was deaf and dumb."

There were tears in Morgan's eye. "Anyway, I have to watch that I'm not always overexplaining things to Priss. And I guess that's why I took to this sleuthing stuff so readily. I like figuring things out."

※ ※ ※

"Thank goodness you've come!" Maude gushed uncharacteristically as Morgan and Sam walked into her office. Taking advantage of the moment, Morgan sat down in Maude's purple velvet chair. Maude seemed too distracted to even notice.

"Start from the beginning, and tell us everything you know about Walter's disappearance," Sam said.

"That's just the problem," replied Maude. "I don't know anything. Walter has a ballet class on Tuesday evening, so I stay home with Jeffrey. His class is from seven until ten and he's usually home by ten-thirty. I waited until eleven-thirty to call his instructor, Madame Louise. It turns out he never went to class."

"So when did you last see him?"

"He left about six-thirty."

"Was he acting strange in any way?" asked Morgan.

"Strange? No. He had his sports bag with him as usual. He changes into his tights when he gets there. He kissed Jeffrey and me good-bye as always, and then he was gone."

"Have you called all of his friends? And his usual hangouts?" asked Sam.

"I've called both of his friends. Walter is not a social person. And I don't know of any 'hangouts' he goes to."

"What about gay bars?" Morgan asked.

"What? I know you're familiar with that sort of thing, Morgan, but what would Walter do in a gay bar?" Maude seemed truly perplexed.

"Are you telling us, Dr. Ross, that you don't know that your husband has a history of arrests in gay bars?" Sam asked.

"That's ridiculous, Detective. You're confusing him with someone else," Maude started pacing around the room. "I know taking ballet lessons may seem a little effeminate to some people, but Walter would never . . . I mean, he would have told me, wouldn't he?" Maude sounded uncertain.

"The arrests were more than twenty years ago, but it was Walter," said Sam. "I'll put out an all-points bulletin. We won't have to wait, because he's a suspect in a murder investigation. What was he wearing when he left?"

"I've got it all written down," Maude crossed in front of Morgan to pick up a sheet of paper from her desk. As she did, Morgan caught a scent of something that seemed familiar.

Maude handed the paper to Sam and then looked at Morgan for the first time that day. "You've had a face-lift!" she exclaimed.

"Nose job, actually."

32

"Did you notice how Maude smelled?" Morgan asked Sam when they were back in his car.

"No. Did you?"

"I'm not sure, but there was something familiar. I think it was what I smelled last night when I was attacked."

"Her perfume?"

"No. Sort of a medicinal smell."

"Well, you were in a hospital parking lot last night."

"I don't think it had anything to do with the hospital," Morgan was staring straight ahead. She turned in her seat to look Sam in the face with her one good eye. "Do you think Maude could have attacked me last night?"

Sam stared back. "You tell me. Could it have been her?"

"I don't know. I thought it was a man, but I'm not sure." Morgan involuntarily pulled her fingers through her hair. "I wish I could figure that smell out."

"Seems like your nose is working pretty well for having just been broken. Come on." Sam was getting back out of the car. He came around to Morgan's side and helped her out.

"Where are we going?"

"Let's go smell Maude." Reentering the Victorian house, Sam rapped lightly on the open door that led to Maude's office before walking in. Maude had her back to them. She whirled around, holding a knife in her hand.

"Oh, it's only you," she said. Maude looked at her hand, which was still holding the "knife," which was really a letter opener. She laid it down on her desk. "I'm feeling a little jumpy. Did you forget something?"

"Would you please step over here and hold still for a moment, Dr. Ross? Morgan, start at her head, and work your way down."

"What is this all about?" Maude asked stiffly as Morgan started sniffing.

"Just give us a moment here, please," Sam said. Morgan was noting hair spray, deodorant, body powder, cashmere, cleaning fluid, and shoe polish.

"That's it! Shoe polish!" she shouted, and Maude jumped.

"Take them off, please." Sam pointed at Maude's purple, knee-length boots.

"I think you need a search warrant before you can require me to remove apparel," Maude gave Sam a chilling look. Sam stared back. Morgan made a mental note to warn Donald about Sam's temper. After a few thick moments, Maude backed down and pulled off her boots. Sam took them and both he and Morgan inhaled deeply. "This is what you smelled last night?"

"Yes. I'm positive."

"I polished them last night, but you couldn't have smelled them, Morgan. You weren't there," said Maude.

"Where were you between three and five this morning?" Sam asked.

"In bed. Trying to sleep. I was worried about Walter."

"Can anyone verify that?" asked Sam.

"I was in bed alone, if that's what you're asking. The only other person in the house was Jeffrey, and he was asleep, of course."

"Where did you get the shoe polish?" Morgan asked. "I imagine purple was a hard color to find."

"At Ye Olde Cobbler Shoppe. They carry every color."

＊ ＊ ＊

After leaving Maude, Sam and Morgan returned to the cobbler shop. On the way, Sam phoned Perry and filled him in on Walter's disappearance.

Morgan found herself looking forward to seeing the little man with the gravelly voice as they walked into the shop. Instead, there was a young woman who greeted them with a friendly smile. Sam made inquiries about the brand of shoe polish Maude had purchased and discovered this was the only shop in town that carried it.

He opened several bottles of various brands and had Morgan smell them all. They each had a distinctive odor, and Morgan had no trouble at all, even with her eyes closed, recognizing Maude's choice. On request, the woman didn't hesitate to let Sam look over the order book. Maude and Lucinda and Corky had all placed orders.

Back in the car, Morgan said, "So now we know the murderer polishes his or her shoes."

"Her shoes? Do you still think it might have been Maude?"

"Let's just say she's my favorite suspect."

"Let's have another chat with Charlie Frazier," said Sam. "I want to know who polished Lucinda's shoes. Do you feel up to it, Morgan?"

"Sure," said Morgan as she rummaged through her purse, found a bottle of aspirin, dumped four into her hand, and threw them into her mouth. She swallowed loudly.

"Good way to get an ulcer," Sam frowned.

"They're coated." Morgan was feeling just a teeny bit defensive. "Better give his office a call to see if he's there."

Sam punched in the number and talked with Frazier's secretary. "He's gone home for the day. Let's go there." He made a u-turn in the middle of the block, incurring the wrath of a bicyclist and a bus driver.

Sam pulled up in front of a Northwest row house. Morgan noticed right away that the front door was standing wide open. "Look!" she said to Sam.

"Stay back!" Sam ordered. He took his gun from his shoulder holster and, looking every bit the part of a TV cop, with both hands holding the weapon and crouching low, made his way into the house. Time seemed suspended in an eerie silence until Sam reappeared. He was returning his gun to its holster. "Come on in," he beckoned. "No one's here."

The only sounds were the ticking of an obelisk marble clock sitting on the mantel and the hum of the refrigerator as they looked about the house. "What are we looking for?" Morgan whispered, as she followed Sam from room to room.

"Anything that seems unusual or disturbed," Sam answered in a normal voice that made her feel slightly foolish. A quick walk-through of the main floor revealed nothing.

Upstairs they entered a huge bedroom suite that included a sauna, a Jacuzzi, and a large dressing room. Sam started going through the drawers and closets.

"What are we doing now?" Morgan asked.

"Taking advantage of opportunity," said Sam. "Aha!" he exclaimed a moment later after pulling open one of the drawers. Morgan peered in and saw a set of ben wa balls, several dildos, a couple of vibrators, condoms in rainbow hues, French ticklers, and other sex toys. She was curious about a large multi-limbed plastic thing, but she didn't want to touch it to examine it further.

"This makes me feel squeamish," she said. "I wouldn't want anyone going through my drawers."

"Do you have better stuff than this?" asked Sam as he held up a double-headed dildo.

"Never mind," said Morgan. "What's this?" Morgan pointed at a brass ring attached to the bottom of the drawer. It hadn't been visible until Sam picked up the dildo.

"Let's see," said Sam. He gave the ring a tug, and the whole unit of drawers swung away from the wall revealing a small room. More of a closet, really. It contained a wooden chair and a set of shelves. On the shelves were various pairs of shoes, including black loafers, gray pumps, and red Birkenstocks. On the bottom shelf was a shoeshine kit holding brushes, cloths, and several shades of shoe polish in the brand carried by Ye Olde Cobbler Shoppe.

41

Morgan started to reach for her black loafers; Sam took hold of her arm to stop her. "I think we'd better not disturb anything just yet." He pulled the set of drawers closed. "Come on," he led Morgan out of the room and down the stairs. "I think we better find Charlie."

They were heading for the front door when Morgan said, "Listen! What was that?" They stopped in their tracks.

"I don't hear anything," said Sam.

"There it is again. Kind of a muffled thumping," said Morgan. "Hear it? I think maybe it's coming from the kitchen." The kitchen was empty but not quiet. "Now do you hear it?"

"Yes," said Sam. "Maybe in here," he said going into a pantry. The noise was definitely louder. Sam started opening cupboards. When he opened a broom closet, Corky tumbled out. She had silver duct tape across her mouth, and her hands were tied behind her back with an extension cord.

Sam helped her up from the floor and quickly yanked off the duct tape. Corky started to cry. She threw herself against Morgan and wailed. Sam undid the extension cord and freed her hands. Corky just let them dangle as she continued leaning against Morgan and sobbing loudly. Morgan wondered if she might be comforting a murderer, although Corky certainly hadn't been able to bind and gag herself. Realizing that she had been holding her own arms stiff at her sides, now she wrapped them around Corky protectively.

In a couple of minutes, Corky's sobs began slowing down. Sam reached into his coat pocket and pulled out a blue cotton handkerchief. Corky took it and blew hard. "Tell us what happened," Sam urged gently.

"I . . . I . . . I don't really know," Corky began. "Charlie asked me to meet him here. I think I remember putting my key in the lock, and then I think someone must have struck me from behind." Corky looked wide-eyed, first at Sam and then at Morgan. "I don't know. When I came to, just a few minutes ago, I was in there." Corky pointed to the broom closet. "I didn't know where I was. I just knew it was cramped and dark. I was really scared!" Corky started to cry again.

Morgan put an arm around her shoulder, "It must have been really awful."

"I know you've had a bad scare, but we have to ask you a few more questions," said Sam. "Do you have any idea who did this?"

Corky shook her head and blew her nose again.

"Do you know where Charlie is?"

"No. When he called, he seemed agitated." Corky looked thoughtful. "I suppose I have to tell you: Charlie and I have been seeing each other."

"Could he have hit you over the head?" asked Sam.

"Of course not!" Corky's indignation seemed to dry up her tears, and she wrenched away from Morgan. "Darrell said he told Charlie about me sleeping with Paul, so I think he's mad at me, but he would never hurt me!"

"When's the last time you saw Walter Gibbons?"

"Walter?" Corky seemed truly puzzled. "I guess at the last club function."

"Have you talked to him since then?"

"No. I really don't have any connection with him outside of the club."

"Okay. I want to ask you about something else. Let's go upstairs." Sam started to lead the way.

"What's this all about, Detective?" Corky was rubbing her head and moving stiffly.

Sam continued walking, and Corky and Morgan followed. "When we arrived," he told Corky over his shoulder, "the front door was wide open. We didn't know what had happened, so we searched the house and found something very interesting." Sam led the way into the dressing room. He pointed to a drawer and said to Corky, "Please open this."

"I think Charlie keeps private things in there. Why aren't you out trying to find who assaulted me instead of invading his privacy," Corky pouted.

"We're working on a murder case, which may or may not be related to your assault, but what's in that drawer is certainly related to the murders, so open it!"

"Okay, okay. But I don't see how sex toys can have anything to do with Lucinda or Judy's murder." Corky pulled open the drawer.

Sam pulled the ring. Again the drawers swung away. "What's this stuff?" Corky said, pointing to the chair and shoes.

"You tell us," Sam instructed.

"I've never seen this stuff before. I didn't know anything about this secret compartment."

Morgan peered closely at her loafers without touching them. "Sam, look at this," she pointed. Sam and Corky both leaned in and stared at the shoes. "They've been polished!" At that moment, the light in the dressing room went out, and the drawers were shoved shut, pushing all three of them inside. They were a tangle of arms, legs, and elbows with shoes raining on their heads. The more they struggled to right themselves in the inky chamber, the more entangled they became.

"Stop!" Sam whispered. "Don't move. Let's do this one at a time. Morgan, you go first. Slowly sit up."

"Why are you whispering?" she whispered.

"We don't know who's out there. Let's keep it quiet. Go ahead."

Morgan extracted her head from someone's knee and carefully came to a sitting position. "Ouch!" Corky complained. "You're sitting on my hair!"

"Sorry." Morgan raised up her bottom a bit.

"Corky, you go next, and start by getting your elbow out of my ribs," Sam said. "Okay, here I come," he said after Corky had adjusted herself. "There must be a way to open this thing from inside."

"You two sit still," ordered Sam. He groped around unsuccessfully for a moment. Exasperated, he sat down again with his back to the drawers and fell over backward as the panel swung open behind him. He leaped to his feet. "You two go into that bathroom and lock the door. Here, take this." He tossed a cordless phone that had been sitting on a dressing table to Morgan. "Call Perry!" he ordered as he ran out of the room.

Morgan and Corky did as they were told. Morgan sat on the closed commode and stared at the phone, trying to figure out how to turn it on. She looked up and screamed.

The glass door of the shower stall opened. Charlie Frazier was standing there, looking wild-eyed and holding a straight-edge razor.

"Well, now isn't this convenient," he said, stepping out of the shower.

"Sweetie!" Corky cried and started toward him.

"Stay back, bitch!" He stopped her cold.

"Do as he says, Corky," said Morgan, taking hold of her arm and gently pulling her back.

"That's right, you're the smart one, aren't you?" Charlie sneered at Morgan. "You know I could have killed you. I probably should have."

"Why didn't you?" Morgan was curious, but she also wanted to play for time in hopes that Sam would come to their rescue.

"Because I never slept with you. I haven't yet killed a woman I haven't screwed, but in your case, I think I'll have to make an exception," he said, while moving between them and the door.

"Really, that's not necessary," Morgan said quickly. "Why don't you tell us what this is all about. Why didn't you kill Corky?"

"Morgan! Don't give him any ideas!" Corky shrilled and then seemed to think better of it. "You would never hurt me, would you, Charlie? I'm on your side."

"Shut up, bitch! I didn't kill you earlier because I remembered I had an appointment at the bank to close my accounts. I think it's time to move on. But believe me, I will kill you. No one is unfaithful to me and gets away with it." Charlie squeezed the razor in his hand. "You thought you could just go behind my back and screw Paul and I wouldn't be the wiser, didn't you?" He took a step toward Corky. She tried to huddle behind Morgan.

"Corky's sorry, aren't you, Corky?" Morgan pulled Corky out from behind her.

"Yes, yes, I'm very sorry, Charlie. Please forgive me." Corky was trembling violently.

"Too late for that!" Charlie mumbled. "Lucinda was probably sorry, too. I didn't ask her. She thought she could sleep with that client of hers and I wouldn't know. But I walked in after he had left, and she was lying there with his smell all over her.

"Judy was probably sorry, too. God, you just can't trust women to be faithful anymore. She denied it, but I know she was sleeping with that idiot Collin Bates! You just can't trust women." Charlie shook his head.

"What about your first wife?" Morgan asked.

"I couldn't prove it, but I know she was sleeping around on me. I paid someone to push her over the cliff. Waste of money." Charlie shook his head again. "I didn't realize how easy it is. I haven't even had to get a gun or anything. There's always something at hand." He looked at the razor.

Morgan knew she had to change the subject fast. "Tell us about the shoes."

"Nothing to tell, really. I like them. My father owned a shoe repair shop. I used to do the polishing for him. I like to do it now, it relaxes me." He seemed calm for a moment as he spoke.

"I didn't plan to take Lucinda's shoes, but they were so beautiful, I couldn't resist. I've missed her shoes since we've separated. I used to polish them all. I got her started buying good ones. If it'd been up to her, she would have just picked up any old pair at Nordstrom's. Stop!"

Morgan had taken advantage of Charlie's reminiscing and grabbed a can of hair spray from the counter behind her. She shot it in Charlie's face. While he struggled to clear his eyes, she pulled Corky into the shower stall with her and held the door closed.

"You bitch!" They heard the sound of running water as Charlie presumably washed the spray out of his eyes. Then he was at the shower door pushing to get in. Morgan knew she couldn't hold it very long. She heard Sam pounding on the locked bathroom door, but she knew she couldn't just wait until he broke it down. She had to think of another plan.

"Corky, get set to run to the bathroom door and get it unlocked," she whispered. While her right hand was holding the door tight, she reached around with her left and turned on the water full force.

"What the hell?" complained Corky.

Morgan grabbed the hand-held shower massage unit, opened the door, and blasted Charlie right in the face. He flailed madly, dropping his razor. Morgan followed up her advantage by rushing out of the shower, grabbing the hair dryer, and conking Charlie over the head. When he slumped down to the floor, Morgan jerked his wrists behind his back and tied them with the cord of the dryer. Corky had done her job and gotten the bathroom door unlocked. Sam burst in with his gun drawn. But the drama was already played out.

Sam and Corky were still at the police station, but Morgan had had enough. Perry had driven her home, and she was in dry clothes again. She curled up on the sofa, under a wool afghan, to drink tea while telling her family about the day's events and putting up with some well-meant scolding for having snuck out of the house in the first place.

"So what was the deal with old Charlie, do you think, Morgan?" Donald asked as he plumped a pillow behind Morgan's head.

"I think he's a very sick man who started unraveling more and more. Lucinda must have seen it happening, and that's why she left. Obviously, Charlie couldn't tolerate that. When he happened by her office just after she had sex with David, it pushed him over the edge, and he strangled her." Morgan took a sip of her peppermint tea. "You know, I think he really did love her."

"Love is strange," said April. "But if he was really in love with Lucinda, how could he be involved with Judy and Corky?"

"You're thinking like the monogamous woman I love you for, April, but I think in Charlie's book of rules only the woman has to be monogamous," said Morgan.

"And when they weren't, the punishment was death," concluded April. "I wonder how many other men feel the same way?"

"Whoa, Sis! Let's not generalize from crazy Charlie," said Donald. "I want to know how he arranged an alibi for Lucinda's murder."

"Easy. He called in a favor from an old business associate— it was the old boy's network in action."

"And he got his secretary to lie for him to cover for Judy's murder?" asked April.

"Exactly," said Morgan. "You know, he was kind of charming in a sleazy kind of way."

"I don't want to hear about his charm, yuck!" said April. "What about Judy's murder?" She lifted the lid on the teapot to make sure there was enough hot water before pouring herself a cup.

"Charlie told Sam he had had a date with her that afternoon. When he arrived, he noticed the dishes were still in the sink from lunch. He accused her of having Collin Bates over. Apparently, he'd followed Judy before when she'd had lunch with Collin. She denied it. He picked up a kitchen knife and stabbed her. Neither of the two murders were premeditated, I guess." Morgan held out her cup to April for more tea.

"What about the mask?" asked Donald.

"After he killed her, he went to her studio, taking another knife with him. He was going to slash all the masks but instead just destroyed his own," answered Morgan.

"Why?" asked April and Donald in unison.

Morgan shrugged her shoulders. "Who knows? Guilt? Self-loathing? I'm just glad he's not my client and I don't have to help him sort it out." She shuddered. "I really did think he was going to kill me."

"Oh, Morgan," April wrapped her arms around Morgan's shoulders, squeezing lightly. "Let's stop talking about this for now. I haven't had a chance to tell you yet, but your friend Maude called and left a message for you."

Morgan grinned at her. "What did dear, old Maude have to say?"

"Walter called. He's safe and well in San Francisco. It seems he's finding himself."

"Aren't we all," mused Morgan as she pulled Priss to her and squeezed tightly.

Photo by Helen Lottridge

Cherry Hartman is a Licensed Clinical Social Worker and has been in practice for 25 years. She is the author of *Be-Good-to-yourself-Therapy* (Abbey Press, 1987, Warner Books, 1993) and *More-Be-Good-To-Yourself-Therapy* (Abbey Press, 1993), and co-author of *The Fearless Flyer: How to Fly in Comfort and Without Trepidation* (Eighth Mountain Press, 1995). Ms. Hartman lives in Portland, Oregon. This is her first mystery novel.

Other Titles Available From Spinsters Ink

All the Muscle You Need, Diana McRae	$8.95
Amazon Story Bones, Ellen Frye	$10.95
As You Desire, Madeline Moore	$9.95
Being Someone, Ann MacLeod	$9.95
Cancer in Two Voices, 2nd Ed., Butler & Rosenblum	$12.95
Child of Her People, Anne Cameron	$8.95
Common Murder, Val McDermid	$9.95
Considering Parenthood, Cheri Pies	$12.95
Desert Years, Cynthia Rich	$7.95
Elise, Claire Kensington	$7.95
Fat Girl Dances with Rocks, Susan Stinson	$10.95
Final Rest, Mary Morell	$9.95
Final Session, Mary Morell	$9.95
Give Me Your Good Ear, 2nd Ed., Maureen Brady	$9.95
Goodness, Martha Roth	$10.95
The Hangdog Hustle, Elizabeth Pincus	$9.95
High and Outside, Linnea A. Due	$8.95
The Journey, Anne Cameron	$9.95
The Lesbian Erotic Dance, JoAnn Loulan	$12.95
Lesbian Passion, JoAnn Loulan	$12.95
Lesbian Sex, JoAnn Loulan	$12.95
Lesbians at Midlife, ed. by Sang, Warshow & Smith	$12.95
The Lessons, Melanie McAllester	$9.95
Life Savings, Linnea Due	$10.95
Look Me in the Eye, 2nd Ed., Macdonald & Rich	$8.95
Love and Memory, Amy Oleson	$9.95
Martha Moody, Susan Stinson	$10.95
Modern Daughters and the Outlaw West, Melissa Kwasny	$9.95
Mother Journeys: Feminists Write About Mothering, Sheldon, Reddy, Roth	$15.95
No Matter What, Mary Saracino	$9.95
Ransacking the Closet, Yvonne Zipter	$9.95
Roberts' Rules of Lesbian Living, Shelly Roberts	$5.95
Silent Words, Joan M. Drury	$10.95
The Other Side of Silence, Joan M. Drury	$9.95
The Solitary Twist, Elizabeth Pincus	$9.95
The Well-Heeled Murders, Cherry Hartman	$10.95
Thirteen Steps, Bonita L. Swan	$8.95
Trees Call for What They Need, Melissa Kwasny	$9.95
The Two-Bit Tango, Elizabeth Pincus	$9.95
Vital Ties, Karen Kringle	$10.95
Why Can't Sharon Kowalski Come Home? Thompson & Andrzejewski	$10.95

Spinsters titles are available at your local booksellers or by mail order through Spinsters Ink. A free catalog is available upon request. Please include $2.00 for the first title ordered and 50¢ for every title thereafter. Visa and Mastercard accepted.

Spinsters Ink
32 E. First St., #330
Duluth, MN 55802-2002

218-727-3222 (phone)   (fax) 218-727-3119

Spinsters Ink was founded in 1978 to produce vital books for diverse women's communities. In 1986 we merged with Aunt Lute Books to become Spinsters/Aunt Lute. In 1990, the Aunt Lute Foundation became an independent nonprofit publishing program. In 1992, Spinsters moved to Minnesota.

Spinsters Ink publishes novels and nonfiction that deal with significant issues in women's lives from a feminist perspective: books that not only name these crucial issues, but—more important—encourage change and growth. We are committed to publishing works by women writing from the periphery: fat women, Jewish women, lesbians, old women, poor women, rural women, women examining classism, women of color, women with disabilities, women who are writing books that help make the best in our lives more possible.